PRISON PLANET
BARBARIAN

PRISON PLANET BARBARIAN

This book is a work of fiction. I know, I know. Imagine that a book about big blue aliens is fiction, but it is. The names, characters, places, and incidents are products of the writer's imagination or have been used fictitiously and are not to be construed as real. Any resemblance to persons, living or dead, actual events, locales or organizations is entirely coincidental and would be pretty darn nifty.

www.RubyDixon.com

PRISON PLANET
BARBARIAN

RUBY DIXON

CHAPTER 1

CHLOE

"New prisoners to be processed," one guard calls out as the hatch lets out a hiss and our small transport ship opens its doors. "And you're not gonna keffing believe what we've got today." He makes a weird, whistling sound with his strangely petaled mouth that unfurls around each word. It's not English that he speaks, but a strange tongue full of high-pitched whines and nasal sounds that I can't replicate. Thanks to the large, bulbous translator someone's installed in my ear, though, I can understand everything that's said.

I understand it…I just don't care anymore.

It can't be worse than everything I've already lived through.

Of course, even as I think that, I know it can. It can always be worse. In fact, every day seems to be worse than the last.

The guard assigned to me tugs me forward. "Move along, prisoner."

It sounds so very much like something I'd expect a human prison guard to say that I want to laugh…or cry. Because the truth is, he's not human in the slightest. The man that tugs me along has stripey fur like a housecat, except his mouth unfolds like a rose each time he talks. He's short and squat, but strong and with four fingers on each hand. Not human at all.

I'm starting to get used to that, though. In the nightmare week I've had since I was abducted from my college dorm in my sleep, nothing's surprising me anymore. Cat people? Sure. Lizard aliens? Why not. Moon made of green cheese? I'd believe it at this point.

My hands are bound before me in cuffs, my neck encircled in a stun collar. I'm wearing a weird, papery sort of white uniform that covers me from neck to foot, and I've got no shoes. It's a little like being in a doctor's office I think, at least when it comes to the lack of privacy. Behind me are three other prisoners, each one cuffed just like me. Two of them are muzzled, and the one that's not hasn't shown any interested in talking. They all stare at me, though. It doesn't matter that two of them look like dogs and one looks like...well, fuck if I know what it looks like. A marshmallow with limbs, I guess.

Out of all the weird aliens, it seems that I'm the freak.

Another guard comes out to meet us—this one with scaly, lizard-like skin that looks as if it's molting. He's thin and tall and has six ant-like arms encased in the deep blue uniforms of the prison guards. His eyes are like jewels as they focus on me, and he stops in his steps.

"What the kef is that thing?" he asks my guard.

"I know, right?" Cat-guard nudges me. "You're not gonna believe this, but it's something called a 'human.'"

"A what?" Snake-ant-man slithers around me with obvious interest, ignoring the other prisoners.

I stare straight ahead, pretending like I can't understand them. Pretending like all of this is below me. I just hope they don't notice I'm shivering with fear.

"A keffing human," Cat-guard says proudly. "I looked 'em

up on my datapad. They're from a nearby galaxy but it's a D-class planet. You know what that means."

"Dirt-eating savages, hmm? Fascinating." One of the snake-ant's hand-claws touches my hair. "It smells lovely. What's it doing here?"

"That's where things get weird. You got a minute? I can tell you the story."

"You bet I do." Snake-ant makes a weird choking sound that might be laughter. "Let me process the other two. We'll send this one through quarantine check. Gotta make sure she can't infect our other prisoners with some sort of disease."

Great. Special treatment. I'm still not surprised. Ever since I've been stolen, it's been one person after another staring at me. As long as all they do is stare...

I shudder, trying not to think of worse things.

"I don't know what this 'human' thing is, but I like it," Snake-ant hisses.

"Thought you might, Noku. I know the strange interests you." Cat-man chuckles. "Thought I'd seen everything until this creature showed up on my transport. Guess where it's coming from? The story gets better."

"Let me finish processing these others and you can tell me all about it," Noku says to him. He touches my hair again and makes an interested sound. "Least it's docile."

"That's the funny part," Cat-guard says. "This thing killed a dozen Tritarians."

The snake-ant pulls its claws back. "Is it...poisonous?"

"Story gets better." Cat-guard waves the other away. "I've got time. Process the others. We'll wait. Isn't that right, human?" He jostles me with one arm and then winks at Noku. "Thing doesn't like the shock-collar much."

The snake-ant just watches me with a fascinated gaze. Then he shrugs it aside and gestures for the other three prisoners to follow him. They do, and I'm left alone in the room with Cat-guard. He doesn't talk to me, just sits down on one of the little tripod stools and makes himself comfortable, pulling out something that looks an awful lot like an e-cig and puffing on it.

I gaze around at my surroundings—my new home.

There are windows, at least. Even in this place—what must be a loading dock or a processing center of some kind—there are large, clear windows that give a good look of the world outside. I know I should be looking more at the prison I'm in, with its sterile gray walls and the strange furnishings, but I can't help myself. I stare out the windows with a sense of horror and yearning both.

It looks like Mars out there. It's all red and rock, except for one enormous difference. The sun in the sky takes up easily half of the sky, and I stare at it with a strange sense of awe. For all of its enormity, it doesn't give off a ton of light and seems more red than bright yellow like Earth's sun. I try to remember what I learned about planets back in grade school. There are different kind of stars out there, some dwarfs and some…giants? That's it, giants. I remember something about the bigger the star, the less light it gave off. This must be a red giant. Maybe that's why it's so huge.

It lets off a lot of red light, though, and that paints the entire world here in the same ruby glow. The room we're in seems to be a high tower of some kind, and from here, we can look down at everything around us. Gray prison buildings are lined up in rows in the distance, and I can see people moving around between buildings, so small that they look like ants. The nearby ground seems to be covered with machines, reddish-tinged rows of strange-looking crops lined up all around the prison "base" itself. There's a distant thing that looks like a smokestack pumping a gas of some sort into the air, and I can see tractor-like things maneuvering amongst the fields. On the horizon are huge cliffs that look like a red and white-ribboned cake was sliced in half, showing all the layers to the world. It's a bizarre place and doesn't look welcoming at all.

I guess I shouldn't be surprised. After all, this place is a prison. Why anyone would want to live here is beyond me. Then again, maybe they don't. Beyond the prison and the grounds itself I don't see...anything. Nothing but barren rock and soil and red, red red.

Maybe the prison's the only thing on this planet. The thought fills me with a sense of despair greater than anything I've ever experienced.

I'm not getting home again. Ever again.

The thought makes tears prick at my eyes. Shit. I spent the first three days of my captivity crying, but in the last few, I thought that with everything that had happened, I'd be so numb that I'd never cry again. I guess not. I hate it, though. I hate everything about all of this.

And as the snake-ant re-enters and gives me another lascivious look, I hate him, too.

"Back?" Cat-Guard asks and makes a sound that my ear-translator determines is a belch.

"I handed them off to Jajji." Noku makes a slithering kind of shrug. "He'll take care of them. Tell me more about this thing. It's female, isn't it?" The prison guard gives me a fascinated look as he approaches. "Any hidden claws or natural weapons I should be aware of?"

"Nope. That's the strange thing about humans. They're the most defenseless things I've ever seen. Even their teeth are pathetic."

The snake-ant puts a claw at the corner of my lip. I grimace, showing him my teeth, because I don't want him to stick that thing in my mouth.

"Interesting," Noku says again. "But you say this thing killed a dozen Tritarians?" He nods at me. "Is it...sentient?

Can it speak?" As if this isn't enough of an insult, he reaches out and pokes my nose.

"Yes," I say flatly in my own language. "I just don't have anything to say to you."

The snake-ant flails its many arms and makes an exclamation. "Listen to its voice! So unique. And you said it's female. They don't send many down here to the Haven prison system, you know. Not much use in terraforming."

The cat-man snorts, which sounds as odd as you would think coming from a cat. "You call it terraforming on the books. We all know you're just working these brutes as slave labor until they fall over dead."

"No one else cares about them. Why should we?" Noku gives a fluid shrug. "They're sent here so the universe can forget all about them." The jewel eyes narrow at me. "I assume that's why this one is here."

"Mmm," says the cat-man. "Got that in one. So you didn't hear about the Tritarians? It's a huge scandal over at Prefalon Station and every single system I passed through to get here."

"Nope. But I assume you'll tell me all about it?" Noku picks up a piece of strange-looking electronic equipment and taps a few buttons. My shock-collar around my neck pings, and I know what that means—he's activated it. Noku gestures at me. "Move to the wall and spread your legs."

Fear flares through me. I pull my arms close to my body, as if hugging them to me can somehow protect me. "Why?"

The smile Noku gives me is evil, but it's the cat-guard that answers. "Standard foreign object scan, human. Just do it."

Uneasy, I look at the two men. I don't have much of a choice. In the next room over, I can hear voices—all male. And judging from their conversation, most of this facility— prisoners and guards both—are all male.

On a scale of Not Good things, this definitely ranks higher than I could ever imagine. I don't know what to do, though.

I know how debilitating the shock-collar can be. One zap through my five-foot frame and I'm going to be out. Or worse, conscious and unable to move while they do whatever they want to me anyhow. It's best to cooperate, as much as I hate it. With fear and loathing running through my mind, I move to the wall he indicates and turn my back to the two prison guards. I put my cuffed hands on the wall to support my weight and spread my feet apart.

Noku immediately runs the scan up one leg, and I can hear it blipping. He pauses at my knee. "Foreign objects detected inside. Looks like metal. Care to explain, little human?"

I glance over, because if a snake can look puzzled, he does. "I had screws put in my knee when I tore my ACL. That's a muscle."

"How…primitive." The two guards exchange a look. "Well, human, it is my advice that you do not mention this to anyone else when you are in the system. I would hate for one of the other inmates to rip your leg off for that metal."

I stare at him in horror, my mouth dry. He…I don't think he's joking. Oh god.

I don't belong here. God, this is a nightmare. I'm just a college student, not some space-faring murderer like they think I am.

"I'll mark this as a known anomaly. Any others we should be aware of, human?"

I try to think of anything that an alien might not be aware of. "Um…this thing." I point at the shiny silver bulb of the translator that's been attached to my ear. At his nod, I nod at my arm, where a tiny little nodule is under my skin, no bigger than a mosquito bite. "I was told that's a tracker. And… um, I have fillings in a few teeth. Porcelain."

He gestures for me to turn. "Show me." After a cursory glance into my mouth, he grunts. "Still primitive, but at least they're disguised well. Shouldn't be a problem."

"She's pretty docile," the cat-guard says.

"That just means she's going to end up as someone's favorite toy," Noku tells him. "Those that sent her here, they're aware our prison system is co-species and co-ed? This little thing's not going to stand a chance." He indicates I should turn around, and when I do, begins his scan again.

Cat-man snorts. "I'm pretty sure that's why they sent her here. Let me tell you what I know."

I'm silent and unmoving as the scan continues and the cat-man proceeds to tell his friend all about me. Or rather, what he's been told about me through the alien grapevine. That even though owning a human is considered one of the highest of taboos because our planet is off limits to all 'civilized' peoples, someone still purchased me on the black market. That the particular someone that purchased me was a Tritarian ambassador who knew very well that I was illegal as hell and decided to buy me anyhow. That he was looking for a kinky little playmate that he could manhandle privately.

Well, "private" for Tritarians apparently means "three on one." Because in addition to having a tripod-shaped body and dual appendages, Tritarians are also tri-bonded, which means that they do everything together.

And as a human captive, I really, really fucking objected to this. I might have kicked and screamed a bit, and my kicks might have landed square in the middle of a Tritarian's soft stomach. And the force of such a kick in such a fragile area apparently is enough to kill a Tritarian.

And here's a tidbit I didn't know until I experienced it: Tritarians are thrice bonded. That means when one dies, they all die. And since these were ambassadors, they were thrice bonded once more. Which means nine Tritarians died in one kick.

How was I to know that I'd knock out three rapists and their entire entourage in one fell swoop?

With rumors in play, it's been bandied about that I'm an assassin sent by a rival planet I can't even name much less pronounce. That I took out twelve Tritarians instead of "just" the nine. And my favorite—that I have a poison pussy, and human snatch is dangerous to alien skin contact.

That last rumor kept me from being raped in the last holding cell I was in.

No one bothers to ask me who I really am. No one cares that I'm really just Chloe Fuller, a college student working part time at a pizza parlor to pay for tuition and who dreams of a career in zoology. That I woke up one morning seven days ago—seven *long* days ago—to find myself captive on a slave spaceship, held hostage by orange-skinned aliens who wanted to sell me to others for money.

It's been a never-ending nightmare since then. Of course, I never imagined it would get this bad. That I'd be the focus of an international incident. They've done their best—from what I can tell—to hide the fact that the Tritarians were buying a human on the black market, and instead listed me as some other alien species. I saw one newsfeed in my last holding cell and was startled to realize that the face they were showing wasn't mine, but some other stranger's. That's the focus of Noku and the cat-guard's conversation right now—that the Tritarian "killer" wasn't a mazu (whatever that is) but is a human.

Basically I've been sent to this outpost prison to disappear. Me and ten thousand other serial murderers, rapists, arsonists, and whatever garbage the galaxy can scrape up. This is where they send the worst of the worst.

And it's now my home.

THE TWO GUARDS CHITCHAT FOR a while as Noku leads me through a series of tests to ensure that I'm able to be housed with the rest of the prison population. Even though no one really cares if the people here live or die, which is made abundantly clear to me through the conversations the men have, there's apparently a large monetary investment in this planet—Haven—to have it terraformed by the prison labor. So singly, no one here matters. As a whole, we're valuable only as muscle.

And since I'm kind of small, even by human standards, I'm drawing the short end of the stick there.

My paper dress is taken from me and my cuffs and shock-collar removed. I'm sent through a sterilization chamber and inoculated against a bunch of different alien diseases. Blood samples are taken, a hormone shot is administered so I don't get pregnant, and then Noku is there waiting for me with a prison uniform. I don't like the way he's watching me, but there's not much I can do about it. I take the uniform and am surprised to find that it's more or less one big self-sealing bag. It cinches itself at the neck and at the feet. Noku runs a hand along the loose sides and the legs, sealing them, and they fall away to make it a strange kind of bodysuit with no ties. I guess anything that could possibly be used as a weapon will be kept from us. I'm not sure I like this weird material, though. It's awfully clingy in all the uncomfortable places, and I'm pretty sure you can see my nipples through the weird grayish fabric, but I guess it wasn't made for human modesty. And judging by the creepily smug way that Noku is looking at me, I'm not going to get another outfit.

The cat-guard is gone, his duty finished. I try not to feel nervous about that, because it's not like I had a connection with him. I never even learned his name. It's just that…now I'm going to be thrown in with the rest of the prisoners, and the thought's a terrifying one.

"Shall I give you a tour?" Noku asks as he finishes sealing the side on my costume. There's a note in his strange voice that I don't like. Even through the garble of the translator, it sounds…ominous. Possessive, almost. Maybe I'm reading him wrong, though. Maybe he's just trying to be kind to an obviously scared human freak.

But then he reaches out and touches my hair, caressing it, and the alarm bells go off in my head.

"Such a strange, soft little thing you are, human. You're going to be eaten alive down there amongst the rest of the prisoners. They're going to take one look at you and fight over who gets to be the first to fuck that poisonous human pussy of yours. They won't care if it kills them. They've got nothing to live for anyway." He makes a weird hissing sound, and I think it's laughter.

"So you're going to sit by and let them rape me?" I cross my arms over my chest, doing my best to hide my breasts. "What's the point in having guards if you're going to let everyone attack everyone else?"

He makes the slithering noise again. "My adorable little human. They're not going to attack everyone else. Just you. Of course, there are ways to keep yourself safe, you know. If you have a protector, no one will harm you."

And he touches my hair again with one of those many, many claws.

I do my best not to shudder. So if I whore for him, he'll keep me safe? For how long? And how many guards am I going to have to make agreements with? Fuck that. Fuck him. I don't want to sleep with a snake-ant or whatever the hell he is. I don't want to sleep with anyone.

Of course, I'm rapidly running out of options. I ignore him and his petting of my hair, because I'm not really sure what else to do.

"You can think on it, little one." He touches my cheek with a claw. "And in the meantime, shall I show you where the females are housed?"

Like I have a choice? "Are all the women kept together?"

"There are only a handful of them in the entire Haven system. It makes sense to keep them all together. They are not given machine tasks like the males are. We have no wish to break such…fragile and important members of our little community."

Yeah, the whole "female prisoners together" thing is starting to sound a bit like a brothel. Great. "Do I get shoes?"

"No shoes." He pulls a baton from his belt, and the end of it crackles with electricity. "Follow me, prisoner Fem14-H. Failure to comply will result in the appropriate action."

AKA a whipping with his shock-stick. "I'm following," I say quietly.

Noku steps into a glass tube-like thing that must be an elevator. I step in with him, and when he indicates that I should put my hands on the metal railing on the side, I do so. My hands immediately feel glued to the metal, as if magnetized, and I can't yank them up, no matter how hard I pull.

"You won't be able to free yourself," Noku says, smirking at my frantic tugs. "That's to ensure the safety of all passengers. You'll be expected to put your hands on any transport railing whenever you are in such a compartment. Do you understand, prisoner Fem14-H?"

I nod. I hate the feeling of subjugation and helplessness, but there's no getting around it.

The compartment doesn't feel like it's moving, but a panel on the light-up grid flicks back and forth, showing where we're traveling. And the windows show that, too, as the scenery whooshes past. Instead of going up and down like a normal elevator, we're racing from one side of the compound to another in what must be something like a cross between an elevator and a train. I want to press my face to the glass and stare down at everything, but there's too much to take in. The harvesting machines, the endless lines of buildings, the bubble-covered yards that are full of weird-looking crops, the striated cliffs in the distance, the smokestack that seems to churn out endless smog (or atmosphere) into the planet's red air.

"Can we breathe the air here?" I ask, curious. "Is that what all that smoke is?"

"The air is still an unbalanced compound," Noku tells me in a bored tone. "It's going to take a few more years before all the chemicals we're pumping into the air actually do something. Until then, if you are required to go outside—which I doubt will happen—you will be provided with the appropriate gear, little human." Our elevator whizzes to a stop, and he taps the back of my leg with his shock-stick, sending a jolt up my body. "You can let go now."

I pretend like he didn't just zap me and cautiously lift my hands. Sure enough, I'm free to move around. I clench my hands into fists and fall into place at his side, just like he gestures. I hate this guy. I'm not sleeping with him. I'm not. I think I'd rather die first.

Instead, I do my best to act like his petty shit doesn't get to me. I focus more on my surroundings. The feel of this place reminds me a bit of an old high school more than a prison. Even though the gargantuan building has a lot of strange-looking technology that I don't recognize, there's a grimy, run-down feeling to things. Even the halls we go down have a claustrophobic feel to them that reminds me of being trapped in a school or a hospital. Down here, there are no windows to the outside. In here, it's all gray walls and locked doors.

And people of every shape and kind. As we walk, it's hard not to edge closer to the guard at my side out of fear. It's easy to tell who's a guard and who's a prisoner just by the uniforms—the guards are in dark blue, whereas the people in the bland grayish-white like me are prisoners. That's the only thing that sets people apart. There's a hodgepodge of races down here, from something that looks vaguely like a lion to something that I've never seen in my entire life and can't even describe. There are things with four legs and no arms. There are things with tentacles. There are things that look like they're molting their skins.

I can't even tell if they're male or female. Then I remember Noku's words about having very few female prisoners, and it makes me feel even more unsafe.

They're all watching me. The guards, the prisoners that walk behind them, the people in what looks like a mess hall a short distance away—all eyes are on me. It's the most disconcerting and alarming thing in the world.

"That didn't take long," Noku says in his hissing voice. "You're going to be very popular here, until that popularity gets you killed. Most inmates here only manage to last a few years before the environment becomes too much for them."

"What happens after that?"

He choke-laughs. "What do you think, little human?"

I hate that answer almost as much as I hate him.

We move onward and turn down another hall, this one crowded with rows of prisoners. One guard waves a wand at a pair of inmates, leading them into cells. I'm surprised to see that this looks a lot like a beehive and the cells are honeycombed into the walls. Each inmate gets a little honeycombed nook to himself, though I don't see any blankets or pillows or possessions of any kind. I don't see bathrooms, either, and I grow a little more worried with every step. Am I…am I going to be out here? With all these staring men looking at me like they haven't seen a woman in a hundred years?

Jesus. My snake guard and his over-friendliness are starting to seem like a good thing. None of these men have an ounce of softness on their faces. Some, I don't even know if I'm looking at their faces. I try not to make eye contact, my body prickling with horror more and more as we walk.

Noku stops to talk to another guard, their voices low. Both guards keep watching me, and I just hug my arms close to my chest and try to look unassuming. I steal a few glances around at the honeycomb, but every single cell seems to be filled with a prisoner…and every prisoner seems to be staring right at me. The guards talk for what feels like an eternity, and then the second one—who looks like an owl without feathers—shakes his head and continues on his way after sneaking one last glance at me. Noku gestures at me, and I fall into step behind him.

I'm relieved when we turn down another tunnel and out of the noisy honeycomb. "I'm not staying there?"

"Did you want to?"

"No!"

He hiss-laughs again. "Then follow me, little human, and stay close. We just had to pass through those cells because I wished to show you off to a friend. You're going to make me quite popular today, as well."

Lucky you, I want to spit at him, but I say nothing. I have no friends and lots and lots of enemies right now.

"One more detour before we make our way to the female quarters," Noku tells me, typing a code into a wall panel and then pressing one thumb-claw against it. The door opens with a hiss, and I see another series of glass walls, though there's no honeycomb here. These rooms are stacked like big shoeboxes, and Noku nudges me forward with his shock-stick. "Come on."

To my surprise, there's no one out in this area. The other halls seemed to be crawling with alien prisoners. In this room, there are a few guards seated at a bench in the center of the room. They watch the long cells, and unlike the guard in the other area, these seem hard and grim. One has pebbled orange skin and horrible teeth, and another looks scaly and strong. They carry a lot more stuff at their waists than Noku does, and I'm guessing that they're weapons of some kind.

"What's that?" the orange one asks as Noku nudges me along.

"A new female inmate."

"No, what the kef is that thing?" The orange alien stares at me, hard.

"Human. She's been sent down here to disappear. Isn't that right, little human?" Noku strokes my hair again.

I shift uncomfortably away from his touch, staring at the ground.

One of the guards makes a horrible laughing sound. "So you brought her here?"

"Thought it'd be fun to see what our Level 3 prisoners thought of her." Noku hisses and then leans in toward me, his hands on his knees like I'm a child he's lecturing. "Level 3 is maximum security, little human. These are the worst of the worst, and they would eat you as soon as look at you. They don't ever leave their cages except to work, so you don't have to worry about them. But we do like to…show them what they're missing from time to time." He pushes at me with the shock-stick again, sending another jolt through my body. "So come along, little human. Let's go show you off."

Is he serious? I stare at him in horror. He's going to dangle me in front of the murderers? No, wait, the WORST of the murderers, just to torment them? That's insane…and dangerous. I don't want to do it. Already I can feel my skin prickling at the attention I'm getting, and I don't like it.

I feel like a worm being dangled on a hook.

"Move, inmate." He gives me a push forward, and the shock-stick sends a harder zap through my system. "Toward the glass."

I shoot him a look of anger, but all he does is laugh at me. I stumble forward, not sure how close I'm supposed to get. As I move toward the glass, horror builds inside my gut until

I want to vomit. These men aren't kept in the sterile honeycombs like the others. These cells seem to be uncomfortable rock with no chairs, no beds, no nothing. There are about a half a dozen men in each of the cells, and as I move forward, they all jump to their feet to come stare at me. One immediately grabs at his crotch and begins to stroke it. Another pushes his face against the glass and begins to lick it with a tongue covered with suckers.

Noku just laughs at this. "Just what I thought. It doesn't matter if you look strange to them, little human. They'd still fuck every hole you've got."

I hug my arms tighter, averting my face. "Can we just go, please?"

A scant second later, Noku's rough claw grabs my chin and he jerks my head back. He hisses at me, spraying a fine mist of spittle on me as he does. "You do not make the rules, little human. Do not tempt me to throw you in there with them." His jewel-like eyes seem cold and lethal as he gazes down at me. "I run this place. You are just the prisoner. You are worth only what I allow you to be worth."

My mouth is dry with fear. I stare up at him, terrified. I don't dare move, not even if he uses the shock-stick on me again.

"Keep her in line," one of the guards calls. "Make her appreciate you like the others do."

Noku hisses a laugh. "Not yet. There is time enough for that."

Oh god.

But Noku only taps his claw against my chin one more time. "Behave, or you will end up like that." He gestures inside the cell. I don't see anything at first—it's hard to distract myself away from the aliens licking the glass and stroking themselves at the sight of me. But as I look, I see there's a lump in the back of the cell. There are green splatters everywhere, and I can just barely make out a hint of what looks like fabric created from the same material I'm wearing. "What…what is that?"

"It looks like they're eating one of their cellmates. Again."

Eating? Jesus. Those green splatters must be blood. And now that I look, whoever it was definitely seems to have the consistency of…meat. God. What a horrible way to die.

"Are you paying attention?" Noku asks me.

"I am," I whisper. He's got my attention now, that's for sure.

"Good. Come, let us go a bit farther down." He puts a claw on my back, leading me forward, and I reluctantly pull my gaze away from the dead prisoner and move down the line of cells with him. I'm numb as I gaze at the rows of strange aliens, all looking at me like they want to hurt me, rape me, eat me, or other horrors I can't even imagine at this point.

I'm all alone. The sharp edge of it cuts at me like a knife, and I feel like crying. Tears won't help things, but I just feel so helpless and afraid.

"To the glass," Noku hisses at me, and shoves his shock-stick against my back. I cry out as it sends a hard jolt through my body, making me stumble forward. I smack against the glass of the next cell, and immediately rear back a second later.

As I do, I see a blur of blue muscle and look up in surprise to see blue skin, horns, and tattoos. He's one of the more human-looking aliens here, but still doesn't quite look like me. In fact, he looks a lot like a devil with his dark hair and horns. But the eyes that meet mine are surprised.

He touches the glass with a three-fingered hand, as if saying hello. And his mouth curves into a hint of a smile, revealing fangs.

CHAPTER 2

JUTARI

THIS LITTLE FEMALE IS *MINE*.

I know that the moment I see her. Messakah males tend to be territorial when it comes to courting a woman, and I feel no different at the sight of this strange little thing. I do not know what planet she hails from or how old she is. All I know is that when I see her frightened eyes gleaming with unshed tears and her small hands press against the glass, I know two things.

She's mine.

And I'm going to rend from limb from limb anyone who tries to touch her.

"Keffing shrikt," says Cthorn off to one side in our shared cell. "What the hell is that thing?"

"Got a cunt," says Ast. "That's all I care about. They need to drop that sweet bit in here so we can say hello."

I turn and growl at him, baring my fangs. "She's mine."

There are a few angry murmurs between the other men in the cell, but they don't dare disagree with me. I've got the brawn and the temper to back up my bad reputation, and no one's ever crossed me twice. There's a reason I'm locked up with this scum, after all.

But to her? Ah, to my sweet little alien, I'd be so good.

I watch her with an avid gaze as the ssethri guard pushes her against the glass. I can't hear what he's saying to her, but she looks upset. Her eyes flick back to mine, and then she stumbles away from the glass partition that separates us. I lower my hand, watching as Noku torments the little female. There's no reason she should be in this part of the prison, and the only reason I can think is because he's showing off his new "toy." The guards like to claim the females here as their own.

Little does he know that this one's going to be mine.

It's a strange sensation to see a female—especially one of another species—and realize that I want to claim her. The Haven prison system isn't where I imagined I'd meet a woman. Of course, now that I've seen her, it seems like the most natural thing in the world to want this creature. She's small but brave, I can tell. There's a fighting spirit that flashes in her eyes when the ssethri pushes her around. She wants to rebel against him, but she's also smart. When he grabs her by the chin again and forces her to look at him, it takes every ounce of my strength not to go into a mindless rage and fling myself against the glass until it breaks—or I do.

But that will help no one. So I sit on my haunches, watch, and wait.

It's even stranger to feel alive again. I've been dead inside for so long, it feels. From my days as an assassin after the wars, to the death of my larger-than-life father. I lost a piece of me when he died, and when I got stuck in this hellhole, instead of fighting to think of a way out, I let myself get sucked into prison life. Day by day, I let life pass by. I rub the inside of my cheek with my tongue, feeling the disk implanted there.

It holds everything I need to escape…but I haven't bothered. Haven't even tried. There's been no point.

I've existed for the last year, but I haven't lived. Nothing mattered. Each day has been more forgettable than the last, and though there are many here that fear me, their faces are a blur. I have no friends, few allies, and many enemies. Nor have I cared.

I haven't been alive until I saw her face.

The little female's gaze flicks over to me again before the guard marches her away. I watch her go with a sense of loss that cuts through me. I can't protect her from this side of the glass. I can't keep her safe if the guards decide to attack her or if another prisoner gets through his mind that she should be his. I grit my teeth, suppressing the animalistic growl in my throat.

Off to one side, Dremmigan pushes himself off the wall. "You interested in that one?"

I get to my feet, eyes narrowed. Dremmigan's almost as dangerous as I am. Rumor has it that he slaughtered his entire crew because they wanted a cut of a credit heist and he didn't feel like sharing. But we get along well enough, he and I. He's clever, not stupid like Ast and Cthorn or any of the other dozen aliens we're locked in this too-small cell with. I'm not in the mood to have a battle of wills over the female, though. "She's mine," I state again. It doesn't matter that I haven't met her formally or that there's a glass wall and a hundred guards separating us.

It's just a matter of time.

Dremmigan nods slowly and crosses two of his four arms. "Got a friend that works under that ssethri's patrol. I'll see what I can find out."

"Get her name. And her species." I turn back to the glass, watching as her small form recedes. "And tell me what your price is."

Dremmigan chuckles low. "My price is what my price always is. A favor to be called out in the future. Doesn't do much to bargain behind glass like this when we've got nothing."

I grunt. He's not wrong. He and I also think alike in that we both view the Haven prison as a temporary stop. This isn't where either of us plans to die, so we're waiting for the right moment. I've been here a year now, and Dremmigan five. He's a hard bastard to last five here at Haven, but he's still calculating and planning for the future, for when he's free. And he's known all over the prison itself. Got a hand in every pie, some like to say.

If anyone can get knowledge about the little female, it's him. "Do it. I don't care the price."

"Didn't figure you would." He gives me a thin-lipped smile. "A female in this sort of place is a bad idea, though."

He's not wrong. It's the worst idea. But that doesn't matter now that I've seen her. She's going to be mine. There's no doubt in my mind. I glance over, and Ast has his hand down the front of his prison suit, stroking his cock. I growl in anger and run a hand down the long spike of my uncapped horns. "If that's you rubbing your cock to my woman, I'm going to rip it off your keffing body and stuff it down your throat."

Ast freezes. A second later, his hand emerges from his jumper and he slinks away to the back of the cell.

That's better. No one touches himself to my girl.

When I say she's mine and mine alone, I mean it.

CHLOE

I'M SO RELIEVED WHEN NOKU nudges me along outside of the maximum security cells and into a quieter hall. I feel like

I can breathe here, and I don't even mind that he's getting a little rougher and handsier as we go. I'm hoping a lot of it is just posturing. I hope. We move into another corridor and then pause in another chamber as Noku types in another security code.

I shiver, rubbing my arms as I think about all of the aliens in the maximum security area and how the guards just paraded me past like I was a toy. I have no doubt that if that glass was down I'd be a bag of meat like in that one cell. I shudder at the thought.

Strangely enough, I find myself thinking of the big blue male behind the glass.

Not that he was human, or even necessarily a friend. But he didn't look at me like he'd wanted to use and abuse me. Of course, I don't know why he was in the maximum security cells. He's probably just as awful as everyone else here.

That's a far more likely scenario.

Noku takes me down another long hall, and then we pass through another antechamber. My stomach sinks when I see another honeycomb of cells, but this time the room isn't very crowded. I see a few women standing around, and they look surprised at the sight of me. One whistles and calls in my direction. "Look! Fresh meat!"

"Quiet, Fem22-A." Noku pushes me forward. "This is your new home, Fem14-H. The female barracks. You're going to be here thirty hours a day, eight days a week unless you're on a work shift."

I'm a little depressed to hear that. It's sterile and bare here. The few women here loiter in groups, though one or two are talking to guards in uniforms in the center of the room. We don't ever leave here? I'm not going to see the outdoors ever again? I resist the urge to cry. Maybe I can get a work shift.

Noku glances around. He nods at the guards, who are looking at me with far too much interest. "Where's Taantian?"

Someone smirks, a bright pink, squishy-looking woman. "He's with Irita."

"He's going to get his cock bit off by that one." Noku makes a hissing noise again and then nudges me forward. "You're in cell 14, to match your prisoner number. You'll have a few days to adjust to your surroundings, and then I'll come by and check on you." He touches my hair again. "If you get into any trouble and need a protector, little human, you can come ask for me. I have a great deal of power in this place."

It takes everything I have not to pull away from his touch. I won't be asking for him. I just stare ahead, looking at the rows of honeycombs. Most are empty—it's like Noku said. There's not a lot of women here. The ones that are look... hard. And older than me. There's a pair of graying women off to one side, huddled together. It takes me a moment to realize they're not two women, but one with a strangely conjoined body that meets at the torso and ends in a long, snake-like end. The pink female is chatting with the guards, and another with a long, segmented body like a caterpillar watches me, a smirk on her face. There are two other older women with lined faces and gray bodies, and they remind me a bit of melted-looking aliens from an 80's movie. As I glance around, two people emerge from one of the honeycombs. It's a male guard of the same species as Noku, and he's adjusting his clothing. After him, a red-scaled woman slinks out of the honeycomb. She wears a sweet smile and tilts her head at the guard, who puts something in her hand. The moment he turns away, she makes a face at him, showing her hate, and stuffs the item into the front of her jumper.

"Taantian! After me!" Noku calls, and the guard jumps, his six arms waving as he hurries forward. The one called Taantian gives me a startled look before moving to Noku's side, and the two begin to whisper as they walk away.

I...guess I'm home.

"Oooh, is this someone new? A female? Let me guess the species." The red-scaled woman saunters up to me. She's human sized, if on the tall side, and walks proudly, as if she owns the place. Her eyes are a swirling gold, her short hair as red as her skin, and as she approaches I see she has tiny horns at her hairline. She adjusts the neckline of her jumper and gives me a sharp-toothed grin. "Sangulorian? No, too fleshy. Perhaps…Markkad?"

I grow uneasy as she keeps staring at me. "Am…am I supposed to guess?"

She waves a hand at me. "Oh, my translator chip just told me you're human. Completely spoiled the surprise. And we do get so few surprises here." She gives me an avid look. "But you're an interesting one. Aren't humans illegal?"

"I…guess?"

The red woman gives a little wiggle, as if excited. "So, tell us all the juicy things you did to land yourself down here with us."

I blink and glance around nervously. Can I trust these women? Are they being nice to me just to have me bring my guard down? I feel so out of my element right now. "Um…"

"So shy," croaks another. The caterpillar-woman creeps forward on little legs, slinking toward us. "You'll get that out of your system soon enough."

"Get a few cocks in her and she'll be spewing obscenities like the rest of us," the red woman says, grinning. "I'm Irita. A drakoni." She gestures at a shiny collar around her neck. "Or at least, the two-legged version of one. This prevents me from changing shapes."

She seems friendly enough, despite the sharp teeth and red skin, and I could use a friend. I'm not sure how to take the "cocks" comment, so I decide to ignore it and I give her a little smile in return. "I'm Chloe."

"Kloo-ee. Whew, that's a mouthful." She moves to one of

the bare benches in the center of the long, honeycombed hallway and pats it, indicating I should sit with her. "Come. Tell us your story. We so rarely get new females here."

I sit next to her, feeling a bit uneasy when the other women creep closer. "I, ah, I don't know that I belong here."

She gives a pealing laugh, and the others take it up, cackling. "Oh, my dear sweet one, no one thinks they belong here." She pats my shoulder with a clawed hand. "Look at me. I don't think I should be here either."

"What did you do?" I ask.

Her eyes swirl with gold. "Killed a man."

Someone snorts behind her. "Forty-one times," one of the gray women adds.

Irita just grins proudly. "Men are useful…until they're not. And can I help it if they don't know how to deal with a strong woman?" Her eyes flick black and then gold again. "I would say I'm innocent, but even I'm not that good of a liar." She beams at me, ignoring my terrified look. "Don't look so scared. You're safe, my sweet. I don't kill women, though. Who would I have to gossip with if I did?"

One of the other women sits down beside Irita and adds, "I was a professional assassin, but got caught." Another adds her story—she's a pirate. Was a pirate. Another is responsible for leading a mutiny on a space station that ended up getting a lot of people killed. Each story seems to be more terrible than the last.

"Well?" Irita asks, giving me another interested look. "Spill your story, sweet one."

"I killed someone by accident." Irita doesn't look all that impressed with my confession, so I add, "And by killing him, it made eight other people die."

"Only eight?" The pink woman looks unimpressed. "Did they send her here because she's a human, then? Should have sent her to a zoo."

A zoo? I'm a little affronted at that, but she's right. I don't belong here at all. "I shouldn't be here. Someone stole me in my sleep, and when I woke up, I was on a slave ship. Some ambassador guy bought me as a slave and the next thing I knew…" I spread my hands helplessly. "I'm here."

Irita's eyes whirl black again, and she leans in. "An ambassador. Tritarian ambassador? I think I heard about this." She studies me curiously. "They're spreading news that you're a Tritarian woman, not a human slave. Someone's definitely pulling a cover-up job on this. How very fascinating!"

I want to tell her that all I want is to go home, but it hits me that they'd all like to go home, too. No one wants to be here. Not really. I bite back the words. "Noku says they're putting me down here to get rid of me."

Irita nods. "He's not wrong. I doubt any of these men have seen a human, and to be human and female? That's a death sentence if there ever was one." The interested sparkle doesn't leave her eyes. "You need someone that will look out for you. Help you learn the prison. Someone to watch your back in the dining hall."

A few of the women are nodding, and I have to agree that what Irita's saying makes sense.

"Someone that will help you choose which guards are the best ones to fuck," she continues.

Right up until there, she had me. "I don't want to fuck anyone!"

One of the gray women snorts with derision, and the sound is hollow and annoying in my translator. Irita's smile remains, unruffled. "That cunt of yours is the only bargaining chip you have, my sweet. You can try to offer your hand, but that won't get you nearly as much as a tight cunt will."

I stare at her, appalled. "But…I don't want to bargain with them. I just want to be left alone."

Someone laughs. Irita just leans forward and pats my hand.

Her skin is scorching hot, and her collar gleams against her red scales. "Oh, my sweet, sweet human. You will learn fast here, I'm afraid. Until then, I'm going to watch over you, all right?"

"Thank you," I whisper. I'm trying not to remember that she killed forty-one people. She's being nice at least, and I need a friend, or at the very least someone I can trust.

"Now, the first thing I'll tell you." She glances over at the guards who are watching us with interest, but not approaching. "Noku isn't the prison head. He'll talk big, but he's not more than the guard captain over this particular wing. He can get you some favors if you spread your legs for him, but not as much as you think. Of course, the problem with that is that it's already clear he's staking his claim on you. It's up to you to decide how you want to handle it."

Staking his claim? I feel a sick sense of dread. "Are you sure?"

"He led you around the prison, didn't he? Paraded you past a bunch of the other guards and inmates, I imagine, instead of taking you straight here." At my horrified expression, she nods. "Happened with me and with Anjli."

"What did you do?" I ask, my stomach churning at the thought.

She shrugs her gleaming, scaled shoulders. "Took his cock for a while until he lost interest. I've had worse. I've had better, but I've also had worse."

I shudder. "I don't want him touching me."

"Anjli said the same thing." Irita's voice takes on a hard edge.

"Have I met her?" I ask, glancing at the faces around me.

"No. And you won't. She pushed Noku too far and he tossed her in the max cells to teach her a lesson. Last I heard, a few prisoners are still picking pieces of her out of their teeth."

I'm going to be sick.

• • •

AMAZINGLY ENOUGH, I MANAGE TO survive a week in the Haven prison.

It's an absolutely terrifying week. It's a week in which I cry myself to sleep every night, hoping I'll wake up from this nightmare I find myself in. It's a week in which everyone stares at me like I'm a freak show, and the other female inmates give me advice—all horrific. It's a week in which I'm watched every single moment of every hour of every long day here in Haven, right down to the bathroom breaks and even when I'm in my honeycomb bunk at night.

It's a hellish week, and the thought of spending the rest of my life here is completely and utterly horrifying. In the week that I've been at the prison, I've been outside of the women's quarters all of twice. It seems that the prison is an older one, and the drains get clogged regularly. There are machines to break up the clogs, but either they're too expensive or it's far more fun for them to have the female prisoners do it. I'm the lowest on the totem pole—and have the smallest hands—so I'm the one given this "fun" duty. Irita accompanies me to "show me how," even though it mostly involves her talking and flirting with the guard while I work. Twice now, I've gotten to get on my knees in the filthy men's restrooms and scoop out clogs with my hands. I can't vomit, because then there's just more to clean up.

Even in those two visits, we were heavily escorted and even then, two riots broke out amongst the other prisoners, all of whom screamed and shouted at the women, or jerked off at the sight of us. Three guards were killed. Twenty prisoners were killed.

No one seems to care.

It's starting to sink in that we're all just bodies around here, and no one cares if we live or die. Furthermore, no one seems to care how we live, either. We get no privacy, and the women fight each other for "better" bunks or new uniforms. I was supposed to get a fresh one two days ago, but Lxist—the caterpillar woman—decided she wanted it, and I didn't fight her.

It's not just the clothes or the living quarters, either. The ration bars we've received have been moldy, dirty, and I'm pretty sure mine was covered with semen one day. I didn't eat that one. Irita was all too happy to take it off my hands.

"What's a little seed but a bit of extra protein?" she said with a laugh.

Irita's a strange one. No one seems to care that she's more or less a serial killer—something she's frequently admitted to with a cheery laugh. She has an endless stream of guards to visit her on a regular basis and is happy to fuck them for anything they can bring her. It might be as small as an extra protein bar or a bit of gossip, but she spreads her legs for them anyhow. "Cunt's just a bit of flesh," she tells me. "If that's what it takes to get a little more comfortable here, I'll let 'em all fuck me all they like."

She encourages me to fuck the guards, too. "You're going to have to spread 'em for them soon enough. Might as well be on the right side of the bargaining table," she tells me.

I can't be like her, though. I don't care if I starve, or I never get shower privileges, or if I have to stick my hand in every nasty drainpipe the prison has. I'm not sleeping with the guards. Any of them.

I seem to be the only one that thinks this, though. From what I can tell, all of the guards act as if they own the women in the prison. Any guard that wants to get his dick wet just has to approach a woman and offer her a little something. Ration bars seem to be common. Sometimes it's a fresh uniform or an extra trip to the showers (which we only get to go to once a week). Sometimes it's for the privilege of not sticking your hand in the clogged drainpipes. Basically if there's a reason the guards can come up with to screw a prisoner, they'll take it.

It's appalling. And everyone seems to be surprised that I'm horrified by it. Sex is the currency here, and if I want a scaly, insecty, or tentacle-like dick, all I have to do is ask. I don't want any of that, of course. I want to be left alone.

That's a concept no one seems to grasp, though. It's like they all think it's just a matter of time before I give in and start spreading my legs. It's not going to happen, though. Never, ever.

I'll die first.

Today, I'm sitting in the main hall of the women's quarters with the others. We're not allowed to go to our bunk during daytime hours unless we want to take a guard there with us. I sit off to one side, hugging my knees and trying to ignore the noises that Lxist and one of the guards are making nearby. Irita is chattering happily with the pink pirate that has the unpronounceable name, and the red drakoni woman nibbles on a snack she "worked" for. The others cluster in small groups, talking, but no one seems to include me. That's fine. I confuse them, I think, because of my reluctance to use the guards for my own benefit.

But then, the women glance over at me, and I feel a prickle of unease. The anxious feeling grows when Irita finishes her snack, dusts her hands off, and then the two women approach me.

Uh oh.

"So, little Kloo-ee. You are becoming quite popular around here." She grins, displaying sharp teeth as she comes to sit next to me. "One of the prisoners has been asking about you, and many are gossiping about what this could mean."

I sit up, frowning. "Asking about me?"

"Yes." Her eyes swirl with excitement. "It seems that you

have caught the interest of the big messakah in maximum security. Word has been traveling all over the prison as to how he is gathering information about you. Who you are, what planet you are from, who has touched you. Noku is quite upset over the situation because he views you as his personal little pet."

I shudder, trying not to think about all the horrible implications of being Noku's "pet." "I don't even know what you're talking about, Irita."

She chuckles, her voice deep and throaty. She puts an arm around my shoulders, mimicking friendliness. "This is a very bad situation, my little friend, and I am just trying to give you advice on how to escape it properly. Now, come. Do you know which one I speak of?"

"The…miss-ah-kah? I don't know what that is." Even as I ask, I think about the big blue alien I'd shared a glance with. He's the only one here that didn't make me feel like I was being attacked with just a look.

"Yes. They are a very big, very powerful race from a planet they call Homeworld. He has ugly blue skin and large protruding horns. Very tall compared to you, Kloo-ee. Very strong. He would crush your small fragile human body under him if he tried to fuck you." The thought amuses her, and a little smirk crosses her face. "Though I think you would die happy."

I don't respond, but I can feel my cheeks heating at her suggestion. So it is the big blue guy that's asking about me? For some reason, that makes me happy—and a little worried at the same time. I picture him—he's not ugly like Irita said. His skin was a deep, lovely shade of blue, and I remember tattoos and dark eyes. And horns. And muscles. He looked menacing, but not unappealing. "Do you know who he is? The…alien?"

"Ah, sweet one, I know everything that goes on in this

prison." She stretches a leg out in a way that's blatantly sexual and casual at the same time. "His name is Jutari, and he's been at Haven for a year now. He worked on the harvesting machines until he went to maximum after killing three men during a riot. Rumor has it that his cellmates are either terrified of him or working with him. That's how most of the influential prisoners around here work, you see. You are either under their thumb or under the ground." Irita laughs at her own joke.

"Why is he here? What was his sentence?"

"He's here for the same reason we all are," she muses. "Because he was a naughty, naughty boy." She gets to her feet abruptly and slinks away from me.

I'm surprised at how quickly she abandons me—until I see Noku stalking through the women's quarters. I get a sinking feeling in my stomach at how the women scatter as he appears. Irita pointedly ignores me and goes to sidle up to another guard, leaving me alone.

I don't get up. Part of me is hoping that Noku's going after someone else and that he's going to ignore me. The other part of me knows that won't happen. I'm not surprised when he stops in front of me, whips out his shock-stick, and the collar at my neck gives a whirring whine in activation.

"To your feet, Fem14-H. I have a job for you."

Oh, ugh. This might be the first time in my life I'm going to hope for a clogged toilet drain.

CHAPTER 3

JUTARI

It's been days, but I've been patient. I cross my arms over my chest, lean against the rough wall of my cell, and wait.

Today, I'm going to see my female again.

It's been a slow process these past few days to squeeze information out of guards and other prisoners. I've made a ton of promises and even agreed to the assassination of a rival, all to get details about my small female. I'll pay any price. I don't care how much the cost is.

As I wait, I mentally go over the few details about her I've been able to glean. It hasn't been easy; Noku's shown interest in her, and that makes some of the other prisoners reluctant to speak. The ssethri lieutenant is known for his vicious temper and volatile moods, and a few of the more cowardly inmates remain silent in regard to him. It's also difficult to bribe from max, though not impossible. I tell Dremmigan what I want. Dremmigan conveys it to the guard, who has a deal with him. The guard passes it on to a prisoner in the work cells, and on down the line it goes. With each person comes another favor, another thing owed.

I don't keffing care. I'll do whatever it takes.

Through the chain, I've learned that her name is Kloo-ee. She is a human, a primitive from a Class-D planet, and she was involved in a highly dangerous incident that involved several government cover-ups. My guess is that she was bought for her cunt. I've heard of slaves from strange, forbidden worlds bought and sold for such depravities. Sounds like someone got more than they bargained for with her.

I like that. It appeals to the dangerous side of me.

I've also learned that Noku has his sights set on her, which makes my gut burn with anger and my tail twitch in frustration. She's not safe with him. Other females have tried to avoid him and ended up dead or hurt. And even though it makes me want to bloody someone with frustration, I know that Noku holds enough clout in the prison that no one's going to stop him if he's decided that Kloo-ee belongs to him. Given the fact that she was sent here to disappear, she's even less safe than most.

Therefore, I need to do what I can to let her know that she's safe. That I'm watching over her.

Through my connections, I find out that the human female has left the women's quarters twice in this last week, both times to clean drainpipes in other parts of the prison. That's an easy enough problem to create. I spend most of the night watch carefully scratching away the mortar around the edges of the drain lid in our cell's lavatory corner. Doesn't matter that it's remotely controlled by a keycode when I can just pry the entire thing off. When I'm finally able to pry the grate open, I rip an arm off of my prison jumper and shove it into the drain pipe, then replace the lid. It didn't take long for the water to back up, and I had Cthorn notify a guard in the morning.

At that point, it's just a matter of waiting.

"Keffing bullshit," Ast grumbles nearby. He shoots me a look but doesn't get up. "Keffing have to take a leak, Jutari."

"You can wait," I tell him calmly, scanning the glass wall in our cell, looking for one face in particular. "You're not keffing pissing where my female's going to put her hand."

He makes a groaning sound and begins to pace. I move to tell him to stop when my shock-collar whines into existence, and then a bolt of electricity surges clear through my body. I collapse to the ground, unable to move. Nearby, Dremmigan, Ast, and Cthorn all do the same. I knew this was coming, but it doesn't make the pain any easier. My skin crawls with a reaction from the energy crackling through me, and I grit my teeth against the intense pain.

It's worth it for her.

A moment later, the glass recedes into the wall. Noku saunters forward, shock-stick in hand. "Remain in place, prisoners. We're here to enable repairs on your keffing miserable little cell."

Through the pain, I open my eyes and focus my gaze on the ssethri asshole. Ever since I've arrived in the prison, I've hidden my tolerance for the shock-stick and my collar. It still hurts, of course—it hurts like fire is crawling through my veins—but it doesn't completely immobilize me like the others. Because of my big size, I can fight it. Of course, if the guards knew that, they'd up the juice, so I've kept it a secret and played along. I've figured something like that could come in handy in the future.

Like now. I'm able to slowly turn my head to watch as Noku enters the cell, the small female on his heels. The guard's so arrogant he doesn't even glance in my direction. He just shoulders his shock-stick and gestures at the shit-encrusted grate in the corner. "Your job, little human. Unless you want to bargain."

And he touches her hair, the bastard. Fury burns in my

gut at the sight.

Kloo-ee sidesteps out of his grasp. "I'll work." Her words sound unfamiliar until the chip in my head translates it—Earth Human language, English variant. She looks around the cell nervously, and her gaze stops on me. Our eyes meet, and I see hers widen in surprise and recognition.

She remembers me. That brings me both pleasure and a possessive surge of lust that seems to crackle even over the pain of the shocks pinning me to the floor. She's so close that I can see the vibrant hazel of her eyes, the dark fringe of her lashes, the delicate curve of her jaw—and the dusky outlines of her nipples under the jumper.

"They can't harm you, little human," Noku tells her. "I have them pinned. I'll do the same to you if you don't get to work, though." He reaches out and touches her hair again. "Don't make me be cruel, little one. I'd prefer you…willing."

She shudders, turning away from me and slinking out of Noku's grasp. She's much smaller up close than I recalled—I doubt she'd reach my shoulder. It just makes her even more fragile than I anticipated, and the protective need in me surges.

If that ssethri dares to touch her again, I'm going to flatten him, shock-stick or not.

Kloo-ee gets on her hands and knees near the drain, and waits while Noku taps a code into his datapad. A release sounds, and she lifts the grate lid off. Her small nose wrinkles at the smell, and I make a mental note to beat the shit out of Ast if he used the keffing drain while I was sleeping. She rolls up her sleeves and leans toward the floor, reaching in. Her face is expressionless as she grabs a handful of waste and slops it out onto the floor.

Noku steps backward with a hiss. "Not so close!"

"Sorry," she says, but I'm amused at the subtle rebellion. The little human has fire to her. She reaches in and grabs another handful, and then another. Kloo-ee is silent, but when she moves, I can see her gaze flick over to me. She's curious about me. I like that.

She has to reach deeper, and her cheek almost touches the filthy floor. As she does, her brows furrow, and then she jerks harder, then pulls up something that makes a wet slap on the ground. "Found your clog."

Noku nudges the bit of material with his shock-stick and then glances around the cell. His gaze focuses on me and my jumper that's now missing a sleeve. "So." His hissing voices goes flat with anger. "This was done on purpose. Was this all so you could get a better look at my little human, Jutari? Don't think I don't know who you are."

I manage a grin, making it seem far more difficult than it truly is. Ssethri prick.

He leans in over me, his beady eyes flashing. "She's mine, prisoner. Don't you forget that. I can do whatever I want to her. If I want to drag her around naked in front of you, I can. If I want to take her to my bed, I can. If I want to make her life miserable, I can."

With that, he casually lashes out, striking the human female across the face with his shock-stick.

Kloo-ee collapses with a small cry, flattening on the ground.

A growl rises in my throat, feral and sharp. I can't stop the hit he just gave her—even though it guts me—but if he touches her again, I'll attack him and bring him down. It doesn't matter that he could fry my brain by turning up his shock-stick. He's not touching my female again.

"Mine," the ssethri hisses, leaning over me. "You think you can touch what is mine? You think I would turn my back so you could rape her?" He shows his small, pathetic fangs. "That pleasure will be mine and mine alone."

He thinks I would rape her? That idiot. I would worship

her body.

"I've seen how you watch her," Noku tells me. He leans in closer, and his voice drops to a whisper. "I've heard of the rumors around the prison—that you've staked your claim. Your claim is nothing, though. Shall I make a vid of the first time I claim her? You can watch her take my scaly cock."

It takes everything I have not to answer. Gutting Noku solves nothing. I have to wait to make my move.

Even if it destroys me on the inside to not be able to protect her in this moment.

Noku straightens. He glances over at Kloo-ee. "Get up, little human. Replace the grate over the drain pipe and get to your feet."

She calmly picks herself up off the ground, though there is a bright red streak across one cheek that fills me with anger. I weigh the benefits of attacking Noku now. Of snapping his thin neck and flinging his body aside…and then what? Wait for more guards to come after me with blasters and more shock-sticks?

No, I have to wait for the right moment. Even if it destroys me.

CHLOE

IT TAKES TWO DAYS FOR the red streak on my cheek to fade. In that time, I don't see Noku. I suppose that's a bonus, but I feel uneasy. It's like this is the calm before the storm. When he left the other day, he was angry, and it seemed like his anger was directed more at me than at the big blue stranger.

Jutari. I repeat his name under my breath. The way he looked at me…I hug my knees tight. It wasn't like how Noku looks at me. Noku looks like…like he wants to break me.

Jutari doesn't. But Noku also hasn't come to get me for latrine duty in the last two days, so maybe I'm not on his radar at all. I hope.

That hope is quickly extinguished on day three when one of the ssethri guards passes by as he does a headcount, and a strange stink wafts through the air. I wrinkle my nose, but Irita looks alert and tense. The other women, too. As the guard pauses by Lxist, he grabs her by one of her feelers and half-drags her into her cell. I'm shocked, not only at the violence he's showing, but the suddenness of it. Lxist is always willing to let the guards play with her caterpillar-like body. I don't know what she did to provoke him.

Irita makes an unhappy noise in her throat and waits until they've disappeared, then moves to my side. "Kloo-ee, today is going to be a bad day."

"What? Why?" If it's a bad day for Irita, who takes everything with a casual smile, I'm really scared at what it could mean for me.

"Do you smell that on the air?" She sniffs exaggeratedly. "That metallic stink?" When I nod, she leans in and whispers. "That's the ssethri mating stink. They lose control about once a month and go after the females. If you can, you should avoid Noku today."

"Wait, ssethri only mate once a month?" Come to think of it, I've never seen a ssethri guard disappear with a female before now.

"They're cold blooded. Since the temperature is controlled here in the prison, their mating need is randomly triggered at times. Like I said, just avoid them if at all possible and hope that someone else is going to catch ssethri cock today."

My mouth goes dry, and I nod wordlessly. That explains why Noku hasn't touched me despite threatening it regularly. Of course, that might also mean terrible things for today. I wish I could crawl back into my featureless, hard cell and sleep, but the guards on the floor—non-ssethri—would shock me for even trying it. I tug at the collar around my neck, miserable.

As if he can sense our thoughts, the door to the women's quarters opens and Noku stalks in. His scales seem to be brighter than usual, and as he moves forward, I can smell the terrible, metallic scent grow thicker in the air. His beady gaze flicks back and forth amongst the women, and I feel sick.

I know who he's looking for.

Irita jumps in front of me and puts her hands on her hips. She saunters forward, her movements oozing sex appeal. "Hello, Noku," she purrs. "Don't suppose you'd let a girl earn a bit of goodwill today, would you?" She moves toward him and puts a hand on his narrow snake-ant chest.

He flicks her hand away. "Step aside, prisoner. Fem14-H, to me."

Shit.

I get to my feet slowly and take a step forward.

That's not quick enough for Noku. He moves toward me and grabs me by the hair, sending a bolt of pain through my scalp. "Did I not say that you were to come to me, little human?"

"You're hurting me!"

"I'm going to do more than that if you disobey me again," he hisses.

Irita steps forward again. "Noku, listen—"

"Silence, female, or I'm going to have your cunt sewn shut. Understand me?" He turns and gives Irita a deadly look.

Her eyes go wide, and she takes a step backward, then raises her hands in the air. "Of course. Walking away now." She turns her back to him and leaves, even as he yanks my hair again.

I watch her go with helpless distress. I don't blame her, but at the same time, I wish she'd have stayed. I grab at my aching scalp. "I'll go with you, Noku. Please, just stop."

He releases me, and I collapse to the floor. "Follow me, prisoner." He whips out his shock-stick, a silent threat.

Even though I want nothing more than to retreat and nurse my bruised scalp, I force myself to get to my feet and follow him. This is a bad idea, I tell myself as we head down a hall alone. The last thing I want to be is alone with Noku.

But what choice do I have right now?

My unease grows as he takes me onto one of the elevator lifts. All of the prisoners are on the ground floor of the prison—guard quarters and equipment are kept on the upper floors…and I doubt we're going to get some equipment. I want to ask where we're going, but there's a dangerous look in his eyes, and the stink of him is making my eyes water.

I glance around the elevator, surprised to see that he didn't bother to stick my hands on the immobilizing bar this time. I'm grateful but confused. It just emphasizes that there's something very different—and wrong—about today.

The door opens on an unfamiliar floor, and Noku gestures that I should get out. Except…this doesn't look like the parts of the prison I'm familiar with. It looks like private quarters. "Where are we going?" I ask, hesitating.

"Always so many questions with you," he snaps, ignoring the waiting doors to turn on me. He grabs me by the throat, his claws pinching, and I gasp, clutching at them. "You want to suck my cock here, then? In front of the security cameras? Then do so. On your knees!"

He flings me away from him and begins to unbuckle his uniform. I stare at him in horror, but I don't get down on my knees. I'm not doing that.

When he realizes I'm not obeying, his entire body seems to hunch with rage. Six arms each make a fist. "Did you not hear me?" He grabs the shock-stick, lifting it.

"I heard you," I whisper, moving backward until my back

is pressing against the side of the elevator. My hands touch the bar, and I automatically move them away from it. The last thing I want is to be re-frozen there.

"What's the matter? Don't you want to get on my good side, little human?"

I shake my head, terrified.

"I won't rape you, but I won't like it if you refuse me, little fool. You think if you were on your own that you'd be so safe? You think if I didn't throw you out to the wolves that you wouldn't be raped in a matter of seconds?" The snake-ant's words are hard and hissing, his expression vicious. "You can take my cock willingly or you can take dozens unwillingly. It's your choice."

I cross my arms over my chest, pressing against the elevator wall. "That's not a choice," I tell him.

"It's the only one you have," he snarls, and lifts his shock-stick. "If I have to persuade you the hard way, I will."

I stare at him, frightened but resolute. I'm not changing my mind.

Not even when he hits me the first time. Or the second.

JUTARI

"Guard incoming," someone murmurs. "Noku."

Even though I don't get to my feet, my entire body stiffens at the hated name. That's the one that touches my female. That's the one that threatens her.

That's the one that's going to die.

I force myself to remain casual, seated against the wall near the glass. I turn my head leisurely, as if barely interested in Noku's reappearance. It does no good to show too much interest in something or else it'll be used against you.

Even so, it takes everything I have not to jump to my feet when the ssethri guard appears, a small unconscious form slung over his shoulder. I realize he's heading toward my location when my shock-collar lights up and pins me to the ground, along with everyone else in the cell.

Noku steps inside and flings Kloo-ee's small form to the ground. "You wanted to rape her? She's all yours. Teach her a lesson," he snarls. "Use her hard and use her well."

And with that, he turns and leaves.

The glass slides back into place between one breath and the next, and there's a breathless pause between all of us in the cell. Cthorn is the first to get to his feet, and he takes a step toward Kloo-ee's unmoving body.

"Don't," I warn him in a low tone.

He freezes in place and then drops to a crouch, watching me.

They're all watching me.

I glance at the guards, but they're watching Noku leave. I move toward Kloo-ee and turn her over. Marks from the shock-stick cover her face and neck. Her face is swollen and purple from the beating he's given her, and as she rolls flat onto her back, I can see additional dark bruises on her skin through the pale material of her jumper.

He's beaten her badly.

Rage blisters through my brain. I'm going to make Noku pay for this. I'm going to rip the scaly skin from his body while he's still living and stuff it down his keffing throat. To treat a female like this is unconscionable. To treat my female like this will result in a slow and painful death.

I carefully gather her into my arms and pull her against my chest. As I do, I glance at the others over my shoulder. "She's mine. No one gets a turn but me. I'll keffing bite off any hand that tries to touch my property. Understand?"

Silence. Someone whines in the back, "You won't share?"

"Mesakkah don't share," Dremmigan says with an amused snort. "Use your hand." He gives me a curious look but says nothing.

Let them think I'm simply greedy. Better that than for them to think I've got as big a soft spot as I do for this little female. Noku threw her down here so we could destroy her. He clearly hates her now, and I suspect the female refused him. If that's the case, I'm going to have to make it look as if I'm using her and using her hard in order to satisfy his desire for revenge.

But first my female needs to wake up so I can tend to her wounds and let her know that she's safe with me.

I retreat to a back corner of the cell with her, my back to the glass. I should undress her to see how bad her wounds are, but I know doing so will frighten her if she wakes up and finds herself naked with me. Then again, maybe her fright will make this more convincing.

But I can't bring myself to do it. I can't harm my female. And I'm strong enough to protect her from the others in the cell, so it doesn't matter. I'm not worried about them. I'm worried about the guards taking her away from me. If she's in my arms, I can protect her.

If she's with Noku, I'm helpless to aid her.

I touch her bruised, delicate face, the soft mouth, the long lashes. She's the most beautiful thing I've ever seen, even now. Her hair is silky against my skin, and she's curiously soft all over, without a single protective ridge on her body. Too soft, my female. It only makes me want to protect her more. I trace a finger along the curve of one small ear, hating the ugly, cut-rate translator that's been carelessly stapled into the soft parts of her ear. Whoever put this in was too cheap to give her the language implant chip that all other space-faring races use regularly. Slavers did this, I'm guessing. The moment we're free of this place, I'm going to fix that for her. She deserves better than a piece of tin gadgetry that hangs off her head.

She deserves better than all of this.

"What are you going to do with her, Jutari?" Ast asks, twitchy. His gaze is on my female, and as I watch, his hand steals to his crotch.

"Whatever I want," I growl at him. "And you'd better not be fucking touching your cock to my woman."

He freezes, then puts both of his hands up in the air. "Nope. Wouldn't do that."

"Same goes for all of you," I say, glaring at the faces watching her. "No one jerks off to her. If I see so much as one drop of cum touch my female and it's not my cum, I'm going to rip your cock off and feed it down your throat."

Someone blanches. Another backs away. Good. They know I can back up my threats. I've killed at least three men since arriving here at Haven. I can easily kill a few more.

All they need to do is look at my female wrong and they're dead.

CHAPTER 4

CHLOE

EVERYTHING HURTS.

I groan slowly, coming to in a throb of pain. Flashes of memory creep in as the pain does—Noku whipping me with his shock-stick, over and over again. Kicking me as I collapse in the elevator. Screaming at me because I won't willingly spread my legs for him.

Then nothing.

There's a heavy, warm weight against my side, and breath against my neck. I freeze, afraid to open my eyes. Is this Irita? Noku? Worse? What happened to me while I was out? I mentally catalog my injuries—everything aches, but I don't feel pain in my pussy, so I don't think I was raped.

I hope.

"I can feel you waking up," a low voice murmurs in my ear. "Don't get up just yet or we'll have to put on a show."

Put on a show? Maybe my brains are scrambled from the beating, but I don't know who this is or what he's talking about. I lick my lips, but that's painful. One of them feels swollen and hot. "Um…who are you?"

"Sav Jutari Bakhtavis," comes the soft voice. "But you can call me Jutari."

Jutari. The big blue guy. My eyes snap open, and I glance around. I can see a hint of blue skin and feel a heavy arm thrown over my chest.

What…what am I doing here? With him? "I…I don't understand," I admit after a moment. "How did I get here?"

"Noku threw you in with us. Said we should use you hard."

I begin to tremble at that, remembering Noku's anger, his metallic stink, the painful strikes of the shock-stick. He… he's thrown me in with the maximum security prisoners? Because I wouldn't sleep with him?

Use me hard?

You can take my cock willingly or you can take dozens unwillingly.

He wants them to kill me. Oh god. I'm so scared I feel faint.

Jutari senses my fear. "I'm not going to hurt you, but I'm going to have to make it look like I'm claiming you in front of the others. Just go along with it, all right? And if you have to cry, cry. It'll make it more believable."

"Gee, thanks."

I'm a little shocked when he grabs the collar of my uniform and tears at it, dragging the material open and revealing my breasts. I gasp and reach up to stop him, but he bats my hands away. What the fuck? I'm starting to panic.

He gives a loud groan and buries his face against my neck. "Sorry," he murmurs in a near inaudible voice. "Have to make it look good to the others. Hate me later if you must."

This is all part of his plan? I—I hate this plan! I give another cry as he rips my jumper further, all the way down to the crotch. I can't stop the sob that rises in my throat. When he said he had to make it good, I didn't think he meant this.

"Whatcha doing, Jutari?" comes a voice off to one side.

The big blue male covering me with his body snarls, his horns looking like deadly weapons as he moves his head. "Back the kef off, Ast."

"Got it." The other male moves away, and as he does, I can hear the murmur of others. Everyone's watching us.

God. This is a nightmare. I want to close my eyes, but I don't dare. Instead, I just stare in horror at the big blue male on top of me.

Jutari meets my eyes and undoes the front of his jumper. There's a thump nearby, and he growls low again, revealing sharp fangs. He tilts his head, glancing over his shoulder. "Did I say anyone could watch?"

There's a subtle menace in his voice that makes me shiver. The others in the cell shuffle, and then it's silent. Jutari gives a grunt, as if finally approving, and then settles his hips on top of me.

I feel the hot press of flesh against mine and realize he's naked. Oh my god. Also, there's something hard pressing against my pussy that isn't...human anatomy. I give a little squeal of shock and beat a fist against his shoulder again, but he smacks my hand away once more as if I'm nothing. "Fight if you like," he tells me in a louder voice. "Just makes my cock harder."

"I hate you for doing this," I tell him.

He grunts and grabs my bare leg, hitching it around his hips. My jumper has practically fallen off my body at this point, and I'm naked under him. His body is angled strategically over mine, though, and when he settles his weight on top of me, I'm practically covered in a blanket of blue muscle.

A split second later, he grunts, and his hips surge against mine.

I suck in a breath, startled. I felt his cock push against my thighs, but he's not inside me. Terrified, I wait for him to correct himself, to adjust things and sink deep and rape me. He does adjust himself, and the next time he pushes, I can feel the fabric of his jumper slide against my pussy.

He's...deliberately blocking his dick from entering me. Like he said, this is all a show for the benefit of the others in the cell.

I choke out another sob again, though this one might be relief.

"Cry all you want," he says, and surges against me again. He keeps thrusting against me, hard enough to make my legs flail against his hips and my breasts jiggle. Our bodies are making a rather loud slapping noise, and it's awfully quiet in the cell. I'm both mortified at the situation and horrified that it's come to this.

On top of me, Jutari gives a loud grunt and then one last, long surge against my pussy, pressing hard as if emptying himself into me. I feel my cheeks heat with embarrassment as he collapses on top of me, holding on to my leg as if determined to keep me wrapped around him.

"Sorry," he whispers against my neck. "Have to stake my claim on you or they're all going to try and get a piece."

"O-okay," I whisper back. I give a mock-push at his shoulder, trying to make it look good, I guess.

He slaps my thigh. "Behave or you'll get a second round even sooner."

I squeak with alarm at that, and someone in the distance laughs, which makes me even more horrified. There's no privacy here. I've been thrown in with a bunch of killers—murderers and rapists of the worst kind—and they're all going to expect a turn unless Jutari can save me. I start feeling panic rise all over again.

He grabs a handful of my hair and tilts my head back, startling me. "Calm down." His voice is calm, but not too quiet, and I wonder if this is the real Jutari or the pretend-rapist-Jutari.

I guess it doesn't matter. Having a panic attack in this cell wouldn't do me any good. I swallow hard and nod.

"You belong to me," he says in that same tone, still holding my hair in that way that forces me to make eye contact with him. "You look at another male in this cell and I'm going to rip his cock off. If another touches you, you tell me and he'll be murdered within the hour. You belong to Jutari, and Jutari alone. Your cunt is my property. Understand?"

How utterly barbaric. I give a little nod.

"Say it," he demands.

"I-I belong to Jutari and Jutari alone."

"And?"

"And m-my cunt is your property." My eyes are wide as I gaze up at him.

"Good." He yawns and palms one of my breasts, and I'm startled to feel the nipple harden at his touch. Oh my god, is that throbbing in my pulse because I'm turned on despite myself? That is so sick in the head…

And yet…I can't deny that it's there. It must be adrenaline making me respond. It's certainly not because a dozen horny potential rapists are staring, waiting for their chance. Ugh.

Things in the cell quiet down. Jutari doesn't seem like he's in any hurry to get off of me, and after a few minutes, his hand begins to stroke my bare thigh up and down once more. He's watching me with a leisurely, possessive sort of gaze that makes my stomach do somersaults, and occasionally glances up to growl at the others just in case they're watching. He's making it clear that he's not allowing anyone to get pleasure from me being here.

It's kind of sweet…but I just hope he can back up that sort of thing. If they all rebel against him and take him down? I'll be gang-raped.

Someone else must be thinking along the same lines, because a hand jerks at Jutari's massive shoulder. "Share that piece of ass, friend. We'd hate to take her from you."

The growl in Jutari's throat is menacing. "Didn't I say she was mine? Haven't I made that clear since she arrived here?"

He has? I'm surprised to hear that, but it reminds me that Irita said he was asking about me. That the information had made it back to Noku and that was partially why he was so upset at me. Like I've encouraged any of this? I shouldn't be happy to hear that at all, but I feel a strange sense of pleasure that Jutari's claimed me as his since the moment he saw me.

All this Stockholm syndrome must be getting to me.

"Just thinking you should share, is all," the green-skinned alien says. His voice is deep and frightening, and his skin is knobby and wart-covered. The eyes that watch me are avid and frightening, and he licks his lips with a fat black tongue. "We'd all like a taste."

Jutari lifts himself off of me and throws his jumper down over me. "Cover yourself. That pussy's only for my eyes. Got it?"

I nod wordlessly, sitting up and hugging the clothing to me.

He stretches to his full height and tilts his head back and forth, as if working out the kinks in his body. Slowly he moves forward.

The green alien takes a few steps backward, uncertain. He glances at the other aliens in the cell, but no one will meet his eyes. "Now, Jutari," he begins. "All we're askin' for is a taste—"

The fist that plows into the green alien's face is a blur. I swallow back the little scream that threatens to erupt from my throat. Jutari's large body slams the green alien against one of the stone walls and his fist slams into the alien's face again. And again. The green pushes against him, and one big hand slams into Jutari's chest. There's a loud crack, and the green alien howls with pain, holding his hand. That doesn't stop Jutari, though. The big blue demon pins him against the wall and slams his fist into the creature's face once more. Then again. Over and over, he pummels the alien's face in a savage display of brutality. I'm utterly shocked at the display. How can he be so kind to me and so completely ruthless otherwise?

The green alien slumps to the ground, and still Jutari doesn't get off of him. He hovers over him, his fist slamming into the other man's face yet again. Blood flies, spattering the dark blue skin, but still Jutari doesn't stop.

I'm so transfixed with the fight that I don't notice another alien is creeping up next to me. A tentacle brushes over my bare shoulder and then slides down over my breast. I scream in horror, batting it away even as the man pushes me over, trying to knock me onto my hands and knees. He's attacking me while Jutari is distracted.

A snarl of rage echoes in the cell, and the alien is knocked aside. I watch as Jutari grabs him by the tentacle—attached to his face—and flings him across the room. The tentacle snaps in a shower of goo, and the creature collapses, holding his face.

Jutari barely looks winded. He's splattered with blood, but none of it seems to be his. He wipes a hand across his cheek, gazes coolly at the smears, and then turns to look at the others in the cell. He's completely naked, his tail flicking back and forth across a tight blue butt with clear agitation. "Anyone else want to fight?" Silence. "Anyone else think I should keffing share?"

It's utterly quiet. No one makes eye contact with him—or me.

Jutari grunts, pleased. He turns back toward me, and I get a full-frontal view of the man's equipment. His big blue chest is heavily plated, I see, something I hadn't noticed when he was, ahem, on top of me. His arms look like they're covered in thick natural body plates as well, and I see more of them on his thighs and brow. I thought they were just ridges, but judging from the crack that the green alien's hand made, I guess they're natural body armor of some kind. He's in fantastic shape, too—not an ounce of fat on him, and his thighs are enormous and strong. His stomach is a rippling six-pack, and his obliques are so defined that you could see them in the dark. Most startling is his male equipment, though.

Maybe it's the wide-eyed human in me, but I didn't expect alien dick to look so…different. Jutari's a big guy—at least seven feet tall, not including the horns—and his enormous dick reflects that. He's not cut, but that's not the thing that keeps me staring. Nor is it the sheer size and girth of him.

He's got ridges all down his hard, erect length, just like the rippling plates on his brow, his arms, and his chest. Something tells me the ones on his junk feel rather different than the ones on his arms, and I shiver at the sight of them.

That's not the weirdest thing, though. He's got a hard, knobby protrusion about the size of a thumb just above his cock, and that's something I've never seen before in my life. I have no idea what it would be used for, and I can't stop staring.

Jutari pretends not to notice my gawking. He moves back to my side, puts a gentle hand on my shoulder, and pushes me back down to the floor. "Spread your legs," he commands me.

I suck in a breath, clutching the uniform to my body as I lie back. Jutari "mounts" me again—and I notice his skin is soft like velvet—and begins to simulate sex once more, grabbing my leg and hitching it up against his hip.

This time, when he's "done," no one comes over to ask for a turn.

JUTARI

OVER THE COURSE OF THE night, I mount the female human a good seven or eight times to let the others know that she's mine and I don't intend on tiring of her. No one else challenges my claim, not after the beating I gave Zzixl and Tkarl. Good. Noku doesn't return either. If he watches any of the security feeds from the cell, he'd see me claiming the human over and over again, which is just what I want him to see.

There's no privacy to take the woman aside and comfort her, so I hope she understands that this display of force is necessary to ensure her safety.

She's a brave little thing, though, and I feel a swell of pride as I watch her small, bruised face as she sleeps. She hasn't protested my "claiming" of her and has even made feeble struggles to make the deception look real. She's smart enough to know that I'm keeping her safe this way, and if my cock's hard as I rub it against her cunt, I'm not going to abuse my position.

No matter how much I want to sink into her, I won't. But I can't help if my shaft responds to her warmth, and the precum that slicks the head of my cock just adds to the deception.

It's early in the morning, and I know she must be exhausted and hurting. She dozes fitfully, her body tucked against the wall with my bigger form on the outside, protecting her from the others. I don't sleep. I'm expecting someone to try something again, for a shiv to end up between my ribs the moment I close my eyes. A female, especially one as attractive as this one, is worth dying for.

I won't sleep as long as I know she's not safe. My own safety is only worthwhile as long as I can protect her.

Even though I've always had a plan to escape, ever since I arrived here, I wasn't sure I cared enough to try. It always seemed wiser to bide my time and look for better opportunities.

With Kloo-ee here, though, I have something worth fighting for. Worth protecting.

Worth escaping for.

Because I can survive here, but she can't. It doesn't matter how "gently" I treat her, something's going to give at some point. I'm going to have to sleep. A bigger, badder bastard than me might be transferred to my cell.

Noku might decide he wants her back.

I need to get her out of here, and the sooner the better.

I rub my tongue over the small disk implanted on the inside of my cheek. It's made of illegal, non-detectable material that scanners can't trace. It's my "emergency" out and is something I had worked up when I started my mercenary stint. I knew at some point, shit would catch up to me. Shit always does. So I created a bug-out kit of data—a tracker with information for a new identity, a boat-load of credits to start my new life, and a ready-made message to go out to my brother (and fellow pirate) Kivian the moment I'm free. He's family. He'll come for me. I've bailed his ass out of shady situations before, and he can repay the favor by picking me up from the surface of this shitball of a planet the moment I break free from the prison confines.

Well, picking me and my girl up, I amend, and stroke a hand down the female's arm, feeling a surge of possessive lust. She may not know it yet, but I plan on keeping her even after we're gone from this place.

Her eyes open, and I'm struck by how unusual and lovely they are. She blinks in surprise, and then her body stiffens as she realizes where she's at.

I put a finger to my lips, indicating quiet, and then stroke her arm again. I can feel the prickle of eyes watching us, so I casually cup her breast and rub my thumb over the soft nipple. She's built differently than messakah females, and I love how soft she is. She tries to push my hand away, but I flick her hand aside and return to toying with her breast. Even though the situation is a frightening one for her, she responds to my touch, her little nipple stiffening as I rub it. Her breathing grows sharp, shallow, and the look in her eyes worried.

She knows she's responding, and she's not sure she likes it.

I need to stake my claim on her fully, though, and if it means touching her all over, it's a task I'll gladly endure. "Do your bruises hurt?" Her face is swollen and discolored, along with her shoulders and stomach. The sight of her injuries makes my anger rise. I'm going to kill Noku, I decide. Painfully.

"Of course they hurt," she whispers angrily. "They're bruises." She peeks over my shoulder and then looks back at me. "Can you take your hand off my boob?"

"Not if you want to stay safe."

"I don't like it," she says, dropping her voice lower so no one can hear her but me.

"I think the problem is that you do like it, and you don't want to," I murmur. "But you're going to have to belong to me in all ways, my pet, if I'm to keep you safe."

She makes a face, and I bite back the urge to laugh. When I continue to play with her sweet little nipple, she makes a frustrated sound in her throat and squirms against me.

My cock aches at the sight. "If you keep doing that, I'm going to have to mount you again, Kloo-ee."

The look on her face is surprised. "You know my name?"

"I have paid a great deal of favors to find out more about you." I stroke the smooth curve of her breast, fascinated by her softness. I drag a finger between her breasts, and she's soft here, too, her body naturally unarmored. It makes her even more vulnerable.

"Me? Why?"

"Because I knew when I saw you, that you would be mine. Messakah can be very possessive, and there was something about you that called to me. We are an advanced race, but sometimes we still have primitive instincts." And I will happily give in to mine to possess her and her sweetness. Every moment that I am with her just emphasizes how right this is. It does not matter that we are in a prison or that most people never leave this place alive.

She's mine, and I'll die to keep her safe.

Kloo-ee swallows hard at my words and squirms again when I go back to playing with her nipples. "So you're just being nice to me because you want to get in my pants?"

I want to snort at that, but do not want to give away our conversation to the others. It's late, and the cell is quiet, the only sound being Ast's noisy snoring. "If I wanted to get 'in your pants,' Kloo-ee," I say, and tweak her nipple, "then I would have already been deep inside your cunt many times over. I do not want just your body, but your spirit. You're going to be mine."

"Your what?"

"My everything. Mate, wife, whatever your people call it."

Her eyes widen. "Jeez, you move fast."

Fast or not, she is mine. I stroke a hand down her belly.

"Chloe," she whispers. "Irita says my name wrong. It's Chloe."

Chloe. It's a gentler sound than what I'd thought. It suits her. "Greetings, Chloe."

She stifles a small chuckle and slides a little closer to me. "Is it weird that I'm not losing my shit down here? I think I'm getting numb to all the terrible crap that's been happening to me. Because if I was in my right mind, I'd be catatonic with fear about now."

"What are the bad things that happened to you? How did

you get so far away from your homeworld?" I ask, wanting to know more about her. I want to know everything. She fascinates me, from the dark sweep of her lashes to the rosy nipples that grow tight as I touch her. I stroke them again, and her breath catches.

"It's a long story."

"Do I look as if I'm going anywhere?"

"I guess not." She gives me a little smile, and I am enchanted at the sight of her. As I pet her soft, soft skin, she tells me her story—of the slavers who took her from her home and sold her as a plaything to Tritarian diplomats. Of killing one of them and the others dying in unison. It's something I've heard before. That's why Tritarians make terrible mercenaries and wonderful assassination assignments. Three times the targets. She tells me of being shuffled to the prison, and Noku's unnatural interest in her. As she speaks of him, she creeps closer to me, and I feel a protective surge ripple through me.

No one is ever going to hurt her again. Not if I can help it.

"You're with me now, Chloe," I reassure her. "You're safe."

"I don't know if I'll ever feel safe again," she whispers. "What about you? What's your story?"

I debate what to tell her. The truth about me might frighten her. I'm not a male with no blood on my hands. I've lived a hard life and made difficult choices. I don't want to scare her—or worse, make her hate me—but I have to be honest with Chloe. She needs to be able to trust me fully if we're to escape this place together. "You won't like it."

"I don't like any of this," she admits. "What's one more thing?"

"Well," I say slowly, taking my time to think of the proper words in her strange language. "I was a soldier for a very long time, until the war ended and I was discharged. There were no jobs, so I became a mercenary for a variety of space stations. Those jobs became…darker,the assignments became deadlier. It wasn't long before I killed for money."

She stiffens against me. "You're an assassin?"

"I was for a time, yes. It was not work that agreed with me. I did not like to kill simply because a fat rich man on one planet decided he did not like a fat rich man on another planet. There is no honor in that. I turned down my employer when he offered me another contract, and so he had me hunted." I shrug. "I killed them all and took their ship and sold it for scrap."

Her eyes go wide. "If you're so deadly, how did you end up here?"

A rueful smile curves my mouth. "How does anyone end up here? I got caught." I gloss over the fact that I was already dead inside, full of despair after my father's death. That a life of piracy meant nothing when the greatest pirate I'd ever met—a man larger than life—was now gone. That I'd fallen into the depths of depression and grief and that nothing mattered. "I…was shuttling cargo on my new ship and ran into an asteroid field. Hull took some damage, so I had to stop at the closest space station. Turns out that the man there working the docks was someone that served with me in the war. Saw that my ID was fake and things got unlucky from there." I crook a grin at her to hide my feelings, because looking back on it, I was a fool. "Deadliest man in three galaxies taken down by a shipping jockey."

Chloe doesn't laugh. She looks worried.

I stroke her belly, smoothing my hand over her silky skin. "You do not have to fear anything from me. My reputation will keep you safer than most."

"And when it doesn't?" she asks.

I slide a hand between her thighs, cupping the little patch of fur there. It's fascinating to me, because it's something that the females of my race lack. "When my reputation doesn't protect you, I will be there to ensure that you're safe. I mean it when I say you are mine for now and for good, Chloe." I stroke a finger through her folds, and she gasps at the touch.

I just smile, pleased, because she's wet under my touch. She can say she fears me all she likes or that she doesn't like that I'm a mercenary. Her body likes my caresses.

I can woo her mind. It'll just take a bit longer.

CHAPTER 5

CHLOE

IT'S REALLY HARD TO STAY unaffected when a big, handsome musclebound guy is grinding over you, grunting as if he's busting a nut. Even though he's not really inside me, his cock's rubbing up and down against me, and I can feel its hard length trapped between our bodies. Jutari plays with my breasts endlessly when he's not "mounting" me, and I tell myself that any girl in this situation would get a little hot and bothered.

It's easy to pretend that the others aren't there after a while. No one approaches except one alien with flat gray skin and not a bit of body hair. He brings Jutari his food rations and chats with the guards, but other than that, we've staked out a corner in the cell and no one bothers us. Not after the brutal beatings of the other two.

In a way, I'm glad. I'm glad that Jutari's strong enough to show everyone who's boss around here and that they're listening. As long as he's shielding me, I'm safe.

I just worry that I might be making a mistake trusting

Jutari. He's kind to me, and attentive, but I can tell by the gleam in his eyes when he touches me that he likes doing so. And he said he wanted to keep me forever. I kind of have to pay attention to that. What if we get out of here—ha—and he won't let me go? What do I do then?

Of course, that's the cart before the horse entirely, because from what I've been told, no one leaves Haven. Ever.

I try not to think about that.

I sleep a lot instead. There's not much else to do at times, because Jutari doesn't like to speak when the others are watching. He "grabs" me and "uses" me a few times a day, and even the guards have commented on how often he likes to get his freak on. Jutari takes it all with a silent nod, as if yeah, this is why he needs a woman all to himself. It seems to be working.

But I still worry. I worry every time he has to stand by my side while I head to the corner designated as a toilet. I worry every time he hands me a ration bar, and I worry every time I go to sleep. How can I not? I worry the most when one of the guards pauses by our cell to chat with the gray alien or one of the others. At what point is Noku going to come and retrieve me? What if they decide that Jutari is playing too rough with the others in the cell and they decide to move him to a cell by himself? That's what'd happen at a human prison.

But that doesn't seem to be happening here, because two days pass and I'm still at Jutari's side, with no sign of Noku. That worries me. It doesn't seem like Noku to just toss me aside and then never show up again. He strikes me as more vengeful than that.

I tell Jutari about these concerns, because I feel like we need a plan of some kind. Me being "his" property is a short-term fix, but I doubt they're going to let me stay here long-term. I have a few more days, max, I suspect. If nothing else, Noku's going to retrieve me the next time he goes into snake-stink mode or whatever their mating cycle is.

"They won't take you from me," he says, self-assured.

"How do you know?" That's far too simple an answer for my liking.

Jutari swings his big head around, scanning the prison cell before answering. I watch the others, too. No one's looking in our direction, but there's a tension to some of the men that makes me uneasy. It's like they're waiting for Jutari to ease up on his vigilance, and the moment he does, they'll pounce.

I scoot a little closer to him at that thought.

He puts a hand on my knee, the small movement possessive. It makes me feel better. He doesn't ever act tender in front of the others, because it's all part of the show, but he touches me in little, subtle ways to let me know that he's got me. Sometimes it's a hand on my knee. A lot of the time it's a hand on my breast.

It does make me feel better, but it's still not enough. "I worry Noku's coming back to get me, Jutari. What am I going to do if he puts me in with someone else?"

Jutari doesn't look at me as he stares straight ahead, eyes fixed on the glass partition that separates our cell from the main corridor of the prison. His fingers tighten imperceptibly on my knee. "He's not coming back right now."

"How do you know?"

He looks over at me for a long moment, then back at the partition. Ever so slightly, he leans over toward me. "Right now, his commander is visiting the prison. He's going to be busy for the next week entertaining him and showing what a good job he's doing running this place." His lip curls slightly at the words.

Okay, so that buys me a week. "What about after that?"

"It's not going to matter after that," Jutari tells me. "Because we're leaving."

I'm not sure I've heard him correctly. I pause, thinking.

"Did you just say we're *leaving*? How—"

At that moment, Ast turns and looks over at us. He looks at me a little longer than he probably should, and Jutari bares his teeth at him, revealing fangs. Ast turns away again quickly and pretends to go watch the changing of the guards on the other side of the glass.

"On your back," Jutari tells me, getting on his knees and undoing the fasteners at his neck.

Oh gosh. It's time for another round of bouncing on top of one another. "Um." I glance over at the others in the cell, and they look away quickly. They all pretend not to watch, but I suspect they see more than they want to let on. I've seen Ast fingering himself once or twice at the sight of me, but I don't say anything to Jutari because I'm afraid he'll kill him, and Ast always stops the moment he sees I've noticed.

"Down," Jutari commands me again, and grabs my chin. "Or I'll make you suck my cock." His words are just loud enough that I know that they're for the benefit of the others, but it still sends an illicit thrill through my body. Not that I want the others to watch me put Jutari's cock in my mouth, of course. But the thought of touching him…

Let's just say that it's getting harder and harder to feign indifference.

His words make me drop quickly, though, and I pull off my jumper, holding it over my breasts for modesty. I ease down on my back, and he immediately covers me, settling his hips over mine. He reaches between us to adjust his cock, and this time he pushes the length of it between my thighs, rubbing against my folds but not sinking in. He hitches my leg up on his hip, and I let him manhandle me.

This time, though, he palms one of my breasts and then dips his head low to lick one nipple.

I gasp in surprise at the movement. I wasn't expecting him to do that…and I wasn't expecting the pleasure that rippled through me in response.

He lifts his head, dragging his tongue slowly over my nipple again, and I realize there are ridges all up and down his tongue, too—and that they feel incredible against my skin. I have to bite back a moan, because my nipples are taut and aching now, and I can feel my pussy beginning to throb with heat. That…that's so unfair. "Bastard."

Jutari just chuckles, and someone else in the cell does, too. I don't even care. Let them think I hate that he's using me. The truth is so far from that. I'm annoyed that he's making me get pleasure out of this. I shouldn't like that there's a bunch of other aliens sitting not twenty feet from us. I shouldn't like that we're trapped in a dangerous situation, in a cell together and worrying about what's going to happen.

But it all adds a fierce edge to things, and this time when he covers me, there's a hot gleam in his eyes as he pushes his cock between my thighs and pumps them. He's slick with pre-cum, and the length of him feels harder—and bigger—than ever. One hand presses on my hip, and he holds me tight against him. To my surprise, his spur rubs against the entrance to my core. It's the first time that's happened, and I can't help the moan that escapes my throat when it does.

"Keffing hell," someone breathes. "Keffing whore's loving that. She likes it rough, doesn't she, Jutari?"

Jutari growls and looks over at the others, still pumping into me. The knob of his spur pushes against my core again, dragging against my wet folds, and I have to bite back another moan. It's practically like he's fingering me, and that's so not fair. So. Not. Fair. I don't want to enjoy this. I don't.

"If you're looking over here…" he snarls out, letting menace finish the statement for him.

"Not looking," someone yelps. "But your bitch is making a lot of keffing noise. That's all."

They're not wrong. I'm squirming as Jutari pumps into me

again. It's the most frustrating—and most delicious—feeling in the world, because it's just the barest of nudges against a place where I want a much larger, much harder sort of prodding…and I'm not getting it.

Not that I want him to stop faking and start fucking me right here in front of the others.

I don't.

At least, I don't think I do.

But right now? God, I'd take it. He thrusts into me again, and his hips rock into mine in a way that drags the knob against my core even harder. The hand that's on my hip goes to my nipple, and he begins to toy with it like he always does, except this time, it's intensified. I lock my legs around his hips, ankles together, and raise my body to match his when he pushes in again. Oh god.

Oh god, I'm going to have an orgasm if this keeps up, and it's going to be the most brutal, most wrong orgasm ever.

And I still want it bad.

His thumb flicks over my nipple as he grinds against me again, and I can't help the next moan that rises from my throat. I need to be silent. Need to not care. Need to not—

Oh fuck. I come so hard the next time he pushes into me. I can feel my pussy trying to squeeze around nothing, and it's the emptiest, most frustrating feeling, even with the orgasm ripping through my body. I gasp, choking back another cry as my body locks against him.

The feral growl that rips from Jutari is almost as thrilling as the orgasm, and I'm not entirely surprised when he comes all over my thighs, coating them in hot, wet seed. He holds his cock as he squeezes the last of his cum out of his big blue shaft and then drags his hand over the pale lines he's painted on my skin.

"Mine," he says in a raspy voice, his gaze locking onto mine.

This time, I'm not sure he's pretending.

JUTARI

I RUN A POSSESSIVE HAND over my female's flank as she dozes, her head pillowed in my lap. I'm tired. It's been days since I've slept, but her safety comes first. Luckily, after the initial scuffles, the others seem to have accepted that she's mine and off limits. That's good. I'll fight everyone in the cell for her if I have to, and I'll win. But the more chaos I cause, the more danger I put her in. The last thing I need is a guard deciding to separate us. Better to lie low. The particular guard assigned to our group of cells at the moment is in Dremmigan's pockets, but that could change at any time.

I absently tongue the inside of my cheek, reminding myself of the disk there. Not too much longer, I remind myself. There'll be a chance soon, and then we can break away. And sleep. Sleep's good.

But my Chloe has to be safe first. I can go a few more days without sleep, but it won't be necessary. There's a low tension throughout the prison that we can feel even in our isolated cells. It's obvious in the unease of the guards and the way they carry themselves. And every day, there are rumors of changes in scheduling: one particular group didn't go out to work this day, or another one has found themselves in lockdown. It makes the guards jittery, and it tells those of us that are watchful that something's going to be happening, and soon.

Preferably while Noku's still caught up in a visit from his superiors.

"You're quiet these days," Dremmigan comments as he moves to squat next to me. His expression is casual, his flat, almost featureless face impassive. "Spending all your energy pumping into the female?"

I snort with amusement but don't offer more than that.

His voice lowers, and he gazes out at the others in the cell, watching them with remote disdain. "Do you think any of them have a clue?"

I don't like his familiar tone. "About what?"

Dremmigan glances over at me. "Do not play dumb with me, Jutari. You are far too clever to not notice." He nods at the guard pacing back and forth outside our cell. "They know something is up. They are not sure what, but they are on alert. And because they are on alert, they are cycling everyone through work duties as usual, but with double the guards."

Double the guards, eh? I file that tidbit away. I know Dremmigan spends a lot of time talking to the guards, though I'm not entirely sure how that's possible given that he's locked up next to me. I suspect a lot of notes are being passed back and forth—or there's a psionic link somewhere that I'm unaware of. It doesn't matter. "News to me," is all I say, running my hand through Chloe's hair. She stirs slightly in her sleep, then snuggles closer against my thigh, as if wanting to be nearer to me. Or wanting more of my touch. It makes my cock grow stiff, but I ignore it. I need to hear more of what Dremmigan knows—or thinks he knows.

"Is it truly news to you?" Dremmigan's third eyelid blinks slowly, a sign of sarcasm in his strange race. "I do not think it is."

"Speak plainly," I tell him. "Or I have no time for this."

"All I am saying is that there is a dark undercurrent in this quiet place. The guards can see it. I can see it. Surely you can see it. You have been here long enough to know as I do that when things grow restless, people riot. They want out, even though there is nowhere to go on this gods-forsaken planet." He gestures at Chloe. "You have more to protect than any other. She makes you wealthier—and far more vulnerable— than any other here. And yet you are not worried."

"And?"

"And it is not what you say, but what you do not say, my friend." He blinks slowly again. "I think you have a plan, and I want to be part of this."

He's not wrong. I do have a plan. The moment I get out of here, I can remove the beacon chip from my cheek, activate it, and send my brother Kivian a message to come and get me. And Chloe.

Dremmigan continues speaking. "I will say nothing of this to any others, of course. And I will use my considerable connections to assist where I can. But if you have a plan to get yourself and a female out, surely you can bring along one more. A friend."

That's the second time he's casually dropped the word "friend" out there. I'm no fool. I'm no more Dremmigan's friend than he is mine. We work together because it suits us. It might not be a bad idea to have him assist if I decide now is the time to break out.

I've had this plan for a while now, but bringing along a female—especially a human one—wasn't part of the plan. I've had to readjust my thinking, recalculate how far out I'll be able to travel with another at my side, potentially slowing my steps. It'll be another person to care for, another person to feed and water. Another person to hide. I'm not entirely certain my flimsy plan is doable with one, much less two.

Three is really pushing it.

But Dremmigan's got a point. He's got connections. He has guards at his beck and call.

I might need him. I consider it, and the woman resting her head in my lap. She's far too trusting. The moment she leaves my sight, she'll be raped or murdered—or forced to give the guards whatever they want. This prison is cutthroat, and she's out of her element. It's my duty to protect her and keep her safe…and if that means working with Dremmigan for a common goal, even if I don't trust him, it's going to have to happen.

I glance around the cell, then stroke my female's hair again. "I have a business partner that will come and retrieve me if I can get out of the prison itself and far enough away that his ship can't be shot down."

"So it'll need to happen during harvest duty." His narrow eyes gleam with interest, and he rubs his chin. "Doable."

"We'll need a distraction. A machine destroyed. A riot breaks out. Something along those lines. Enough of a diversion to allow me—to allow us—to get off of the prison grounds themselves." My plan has never been set in stone. I'm an opportunist, and figured I'd use whenever and whatever presented itself as useful. Of course, now that I have Chloe, I need to think ahead.

Dremmigan continues to rub his chin, thoughtful. "And the shock barrier that surrounds the prison? Do you have a method of disabling that?"

"Won't need to. You just get me there and I can do the rest." I can power through whatever pain it unleashes and then drag Chloe through if she can't move. I can drag one more, I suppose.

He nods and gets to his feet. "I'll see what I can do."

As the strange alien wanders away, I find myself touching my human again. I smooth a hand up and down the curve of her hip, since a more tender touch might be misconstrued. I wish I'd met her under different circumstances, where I didn't have to manhandle her constantly in order to keep her safe. She must hate it—and me.

And yet…I think of the way she'd cried out the last time I moved over her. I hadn't been paying attention, focused on one of the others watching us, and my spur had penetrated her. I hadn't expected that she'd respond with an urgent cry, her body arching. After that, it was impossible for me to stop. I'd wanted it too much. Wanted her too much. Chloe had encouraged me with her little sounds and the way she'd clung to me, and it was the most intensely pleasurable experience I'd ever had. I'd painted her thighs with my cum, though I'd wanted nothing more than to push into her sweet heat and fill her with my seed. Get her pregnant with my child. Claim her fully.

I can't while she's not safe, though. I need to take her away from here.

Until then, I can't let things go that far again. Not if I want her to trust me.

It's the middle of the night when I hear voices speaking outside the cell.

"Why is there a female in max with the other prisoners?"

There's a hissing sound that makes the small hairs on my neck rise. I know that sound. "The female is a misbehaving inmate. She is from a primitive people and responds best to violence. Right now she is being punished for disobedience."

I force myself to straighten, watching from the corner I've claimed as mine as Noku and another uniformed officer pause in front of the glass partition of our particular cell. It's interesting that Noku doesn't look like his regular self. His scales have been polished, and the uniform he's wearing is far crisper than what he normally chooses to wear. Lazy bastard probably gives the minimum down here. The alien he stands with—a szzt—looks balefully on his surroundings, displeased. He stands straight, several medals hanging off the chest of his uniform, and he holds a datapad in hand, recording his observations.

"What exactly is that thing?" the commander asks, gesturing at Chloe. "It's ugly."

"Humans. A disgusting race," Noku says. "She is a political prisoner and has been sent here to be quietly disposed of."

The szzt bares its teeth in a grimace. "And they respond

only to violence?"

"That is correct," Noku assures him. "As you can see, she has integrated herself quite well with the others in max. Once she has been properly punished she will be returned to the female quarters. "He turns his back to the cell and gestures farther down the hall. "Over here we have our Angarian warlord—"

The commander doesn't move, though. He's still studying Chloe with a scowl on his face.

I put a possessive hand on her hip, looking as menacing as possible. She's mine.

"Is there something that distresses you, Commander?" Noku asks in his most solicitous voice. "Shall I have her removed immediately?"

I bare my teeth at the thought. If they so much as touch her—

"It is not that." The commander glances over at Noku. "I am well aware that the females in this prison trade their attentions in exchange for amenities from the guards. It's a necessary evil I choose to overlook to keep the help happy. However. This…thing. This human. It could be diseased."

"It could," Noku agrees. His glare focuses on me instead of Chloe, though I can only imagine that he wants to look at her. He's too covetous, the ssethri officer. He's going to want her back.

"They haven't touched this one, have they? The other guards?" The look on his face says he clearly frowns on the thought.

"Of course not. As you said, it could be diseased." Noku's hissing voice is offended. "It is a highly unpleasant creature."

His response makes me both amused and angry all at once. If only his commander knew what Noku was truly up to. Chloe's no grotesque creature.

She's mine.

Maybe it's the rebellious bastard in me—or the angry defender of Chloe—but to have her lied about so clearly by Noku fills me with anger. I slide a hand between her thighs and seek out the warm nest of curls that covers her cunt. I drag my fingers over her folds, exploring her. She's got a little nub here that I accidentally grazed against earlier today and she went wild in my arms, so I'm going to touch it again and see if she responds the same way.

Chloe wakes up from her sleep with a moan, clinging to me.

"Gods damn it, there they go again," someone says loudly. "Keffing human. Go to sleep already."

I continue to stroke Chloe's soft folds as her legs part for me. She's half asleep, pressing her body against mine, even as I toy with her cunt. She grows slick immediately, and my cock hardens in response. I look up at the glass, filled with satisfaction to see that Noku's watching me touch his female.

That he's hearing her cries of pleasure.

The officer is speaking to Noku, but I don't think the ssethri is hearing a thing. He's gazing hard at Chloe as she squirms under my hand, panting.

"Jutari!" she cries, clinging to my neck. "What—"

"Say you're mine, Chloe," I tell her as I stroke that hard little bud between her folds. And I give Noku a sly smile as I do. Let him watch me pleasure his female. Let her grab on to me and demand that I own her, when she would not touch him.

Let him know that Sav Jutari Bakhtavis has taken what he wanted.

CHAPTER 6

JUTARI

THE IMPLICATIONS OF MY ACTIONS aren't felt until the morning.

Dremmigan chats with one of the guards as ration bars are delivered to our cell. He takes the stack of bars, hands them out and then saves two, moving to my side where Chloe sits next to me. She's still flushed and embarrassed from my late-night "claiming" of her. I made her come against my hand twice and then licked her juices off my flesh. She's embarrassed by the sounds she makes when I touch her, but I crave them.

I'm not a nice guy, either, because I'm going to make her keep giving them to me. I don't care if the entire Haven prison knows that I make her scream when I touch her.

Dremmigan holds our ration bars out. When I reach for them, he pulls them back, tilting his head.

I growl at him. "What?"

"Done showing off your plaything?" His tone is cold.

I grin at that, baring my teeth at him. "No. I'm going to

need to touch her again soon enough. Cover your ears if you don't like it."

"Jutari," Chloe whispers angrily, embarrassed.

I don't care. Drem just blinks his eyes in that third-lidded way that shows his exasperation. "Thanks to your stunt with the female, our group has been assigned harvesting duties for the next week."

I grunt, taking the bars from him and handing Chloe one. Harvesting duties are a necessary evil. I don't mind them because at least it gets us out of this cell for a few hours, even if it's just under the red sky and thin air of Haven's undeveloped atmosphere. "And?"

"And it's thresher duty."

I pause at that. Thresher duty is the most dangerous of chores and is usually given as a punishment. The enormous harvesting machines—the threshers—are automated, but they move quickly to mow through the special grasses that are grown here. Thresher duty means that the prisoners are in charge of clearing obstacles from the large threshers' paths, or occasionally clearing the blades themselves. It's not something that anyone looks forward to, unless you have a death wish.

Still...the threshers are in the fields at the edge of the prison compound. If we get out there, all that's between us and the red cliffs of freedom is the electric-shock field that surrounds the prison. It'll disable most humanoids with a single zap to their systems, like a shock-collar.

Except for me.

This is the chance I've been waiting for. I just grin at him, looking confident. "This is our moment, then." I gesture for Chloe to eat and hand her my bar as well. She'll need her strength.

She gives me a worried look but says nothing in front of Dremmigan. Smart little thing. I know she has questions, but she's waiting to ask them. Good. I don't want her to find out that Noku mentioned returning her to the women's quarters. She's staying with me, and that's final.

"I thought you might say that," Drem comments in that too-smooth, emotionless voice of his. "I spoke with the guard, and he owes me a favor. He's got a friend working perimeter duty. This friend is going to meet us with a stash of food and water for our escape, plus extra breathers." He clasps his long-fingered hands and watches me. "If you can get us past the perimeter, I've got us supplies."

I nod. "I can get us past." I'm a little skeptical of Dremmigan's casual reassurance, though. That seems a little too easy to me, especially for something that a guard could get executed for. "That must be quite the favor the guard owes you."

"Indeed."

When he doesn't elaborate, I give him an impatient scowl.

"I told him that we would let him have a turn with the female."

Hot, furious rage boils through my body. I jump to my feet, ready to wrap my hands around Dremmigan's thin neck. "You *what*?"

"Calm yourself," Drem says. "You'll draw attention to us."

I snarl at him. Like I give a kef if I draw attention—

"Jutari," Chloe says in a soft voice, her hand seeking mine. "Please."

Her touch eases some of the fury racing through me, pulling me back from the brink. It takes everything I have to calmly sit down again instead of rending Dremmigan in two like I want to. I sit next to my female and pull her into my lap, feeling possessive. "That's not on the table."

"Oh, it is a lie," Dremmigan reassures me. "He can think that, but she will be going with us. I had to agree to something, though. Rumor has it that Noku's superiors are leaving Haven today, and you know what that means."

I do. It means he's coming for Chloe. And Drem has correctly guessed that I won't leave this place without her.

She puts her arms around my neck and strokes one of my horns. I don't know that she realizes how erotic that movement is, since she's trying to comfort me, but it's making my cock ache worse. I'm tempted to throw her down on the floor and claim her—really, truly claim her—just to show everyone that she's mine. It's the barbaric side of me coming out at the thought of her being threatened.

Chloe is *mine*.

"How are we going to do this?" Chloe asks, voice low. "Do you have a plan, Jutari?"

I nod slowly, focusing on her calm words and not Dremmigan's impassive keffing bastard face. I stroke a hand down her back. "The harvesters are easy enough to jam. We just need to figure out a way to get one to break down." Or for someone to have an accident, but I don't say that. I suspect Chloe doesn't realize how bad of a man I am. She has an innocence about her, and it makes me...well, it makes me want to be better. To give a shit. To care, even though I stopped caring a long keffing time ago. But having her in my life changes things.

It changes everything.

"An accident is easy enough," Dremmigan says in that cold voice of his. "Then we'll meet at the perimeter."

I nod. It should all be easy enough. I rub my tongue against the disk in my cheek.

Then freedom.

CHLOE

IT'S NERVE-WRACKING TO BE LINED up with the other

prisoners for Harvester duty. It's going to be my first time going outside since I've arrived in the prison, and I'm not sure what to expect. It makes me a little nervous that in addition to a pair of cheap shoes, I'm given a thing that clips on my nose called a "breather." Apparently it has little filters that go into the nostrils and make the air breathable, because it's not quite there yet. I've seen a few aliens in the prison with them on, but I didn't realize that was what they were for. I'm situated in line behind the lanky, pencil-gray alien called Dremmigan, and Jutari is behind me. Each guard that passes by makes me a little more nervous, because I expect someone to notice that I'm a girl mixed in with all these guys, and decide that no, I belong back in the female quarters.

I need to stay with Jutari. Not just because he wants to get out of here, but because he's safe.

And because...I like him. Which is silly. Now's not the time for a schoolgirl sort of crush, but I can't help it. When he touches me, I get all giddy. It doesn't matter that the situation is crazy—maybe the situation is part of the reason why I'm so fascinated by him. It doesn't matter, because at the end of the day, I belong to Jutari...and I love it.

I'd prefer to be alone with him instead of in a cell with a bunch of murderers, but I'm trying not to dwell on that fact.

As if he can hear my thoughts, Jutari grabs a handful of my hair and tugs my head back. The movement seems rough and possessive, but I know it's because he needs to make it look like he "owns" me. He's apologized multiple times for manhandling me. As long as he doesn't hurt me, though...I kind of like being manhandled by him. It's sexy and wrong all at once. "Be calm," he murmurs to me. "Listen for my commands when we're out there, and stay close."

"I will."

"The harvesters are dangerous. I'm going to keep you out of their way if at all possible, but if not, you have to be on your guard." He strokes a hand down the side of my neck. "And be ready at all times."

I nod as he releases my hair.

Both he and Dremmigan are calm as could be. It's a little frustrating that they can show zero emotion about today's big breakout, but I'm a nervous wreck. Drem's already growled at me a few times for being a mess, but Jutari told one of the guards as he gave me a strange look that I was scared to go outside. It's plausible.

I'm more scared that someone's going to take me away from Jutari.

We're led down a long, metal-lined tunnel. There are guide-rails all along the walls and a bunch of signs printed with a language I can't read. I imagine them saying stuff like "Keep your hands at your sides" or "Don't shiv your co-worker" or fun things like that. As we walk, my steps feel springier, weirder. I originally think it's the floors, but when we go through the doors and step outside into the red atmosphere, I realize that it's the air here.

It's so...weird. It feels too thin, and I suck in a breath through my nosepiece, as if I can't get enough oxygen. Thin... and yet muggy. The air feels steamy and gross compared to the climate-controlled rooms inside. I move an arm, and it seemingly floats past me with little effort. Huh.

"Gravity here is lighter than inside," Jutari says, touching a hand to my waist. "Be careful."

I will. I follow along behind the line of prisoners as they walk the edges of what seems like an enormous field of greenery. It's noisy out here—the wind batters and rips at my skin, coating me in blood-red dust in a matter of seconds. Over the wind is a constant mechanical grinding noise, loud enough to make me want to rip the bulbous translator out of my ear. I can't see what's causing it until one of the machines moves past us. The thing's gosh-darned enormous and looks like a gigantic bullet with a huge rotating set of blades stuck to the front. As I watch, it threshes its way past us, plucking the grasses from the ground by the root and then pushing them into a compartment.

"What the heck is it doing?" I ask over the roar of the machinery.

"The rootlings have to be grown here. Once they reach a certain height, the harvesters pull them from the soil here and they're planted in fields elsewhere on the surface. It's part of the terraforming," Jutari explains.

Rootlings? I pick up a fallen one near my feet. What I thought was grass is actually a very tiny tree of some kind. How fascinating.

"Keep walking," a guard says over an intercom. "Do not stop until you've reached your assigned destination."

Oops. I hurry to follow Dremmigan's footsteps, wincing as I do. Between the thin, sweaty-feeling air and the gravity, it doesn't help that the soil here feels slippery and loose. I'm totally going to fall on my ass if we have to run.

I really, really hope it doesn't come to that.

We walk outside for what feels like hours. No one talks much, and when they do, it's quickly shut down by a guard. There's more of them watching the prisoners than I've ever seen, and I'm guessing this is where the majority of staff works—outside. I glance behind us and see an endless line of prisoners, all wearing the blinking shock-collars. Lots of people working in the fields today. "Is it this busy every day?"

"Usually," Jutari answers me. "We're just not on the rotation most times." He bares his teeth in a grin. "This is our punishment."

A punishment that's going to allow us to escape—hopefully.

We get to the far end of the fields, and the cliffs seem enticingly close from here. It's been a long slog in the dust, though, and I'm already exhausted.

"Get a ration of water and then into the field, prisoners," a guard calls out.

A blur of red appears out of the corner of my eye. "Water pods," Irita calls, holding up a clear sack the size of my fist. She tosses one at a prisoner and then holds it up again. "Be nice to me and you might get double."

"No, you won't," warns the nearest guard.

"Okay, you won't. Be nice to me and I won't spill yours on the ground," Irita amends. She hands a bag to Dremmigan, who heads out into the field.

"Come," Jutari says to me. "Before they notice you're female and put you on water duty."

But Irita exclaims at the sight of me. "Kloo-ee! Look at you. Kef, your face is an absolute mess."

"Irita, hi." I'm kind of happy to see her and yet impatient at the same time. "I need to get out into the field—"

Jutari tugs on my hand.

"Come find me if you need water," she says with a wink. "I'll be here. Be careful out in the field."

I nod at her and let Jutari pull me along. We move toward the edges of the big field, a spot that most of the prisoners seem to be avoiding. A harvester drones on in the distance, the sound growing gradually louder as it creeps toward our direction.

"What do we do out here?" I ask Jutari, wincing as my feet stick into the muddy, churned ground. "Other than try not to get run over."

He picks up one of the tiny saplings and sticks the roots into the dirt. "We replant so the harvester can grab them on a second pass. And we watch for breakdowns in the machinery." He gives me a quick look. "And we wait for our chance."

There don't seem to be many people at this end of the field, but Dremmigan's also nowhere close. "Not right now?"

"Not right now," he agrees. "We need to wait for the guards

to get bored. They'll be less alert later in the day."

"Gotcha." I step forward and pick up a fallen sapling. The ground is littered with them, the earth churned to a gritty, muddy mess from the passes of the harvesters. As I watch, one zooms past not too far from where we stand, and someone jumps out of the way of the machine. Jeez. "There has to be a better way to do this."

"There is," Jutari tells me as he begins to work. "But we're cheap labor."

Good point.

"Stay near me. If you get tired, let me know. I'll carry you on my back if I have to." He reaches out and puts a hand on top of my head, then strokes my hair. "I don't want anything to happen to you. You're mine."

And I melt at that. "I'm nervous."

"Don't be. I have you."

Strangely enough, that confident statement makes me feel better. "Can I have a kiss for luck, then?"

He tilts his head, surprised. "Kiss? I don't know what you mean."

"Do your people not kiss? Mouth on mouth?"

Jutari's eyes gleam with interest. "I think it would violate several hygiene laws on many planets."

"Oh." I'm disappointed to hear that.

"But I will kiss you." He glances around and then picks up another sapling. "Not here, though. When we're alone for the first time, I'll put my mouth on yours."

I've never heard anything more romantic.

"Rumor has it that you're breaking out today."

I choke on my water as Irita offers me another baggy of it. I'm standing on the edge of the field while the men work nearby. It's blisteringly hot and muggy, and even though it's windy, it's not doing much other than to make me dirty. It's like I'm trapped in a hair dryer, and it's miserable. Jutari doesn't seem affected, but he watches me closely, and I think he worries I won't be able to make our escape. He might be right—it's only been a few hours of field work, but I'm exhausted. When the last thresher zoomed past, I stumbled as I got out of the way, and though it wasn't close, I had a brief flash of how my death could have gone down. Not good. I look over at Irita out of the corner of my eye. "Where did you hear that?"

"Everywhere. One of the guards with a small dick has a big mouth. That's usually how it goes." She shrugs. "I thought I'd warn you, though. Dremmigan's not to be trusted."

I glance over at the smooth gray alien, worried. He started working at the center of the field and has been slowly making his way to the edge. Jutari has been creeping closer as well, though he's moving so gradually as he works that it seems natural. "Did…did you want to come with us?"

"Kef no, little one. I'm good where I'm at. Trading pussy on the outside's the same as trading pussy here." She plucks my empty water-sack from my hand and puts it in the discard bag strapped to her hip. "But I did want to pass a warning. Your partner's not to be trusted. Watch your back, that's all I'm saying." She saunters past me. "And now I have to go. Good luck."

I ponder her words as I step onto the field and move toward Jutari.

"Careful," he warns me as I stumble into a tracked groove. He reaches out and supports me with one big blue hand. "Do you need to rest?"

"No. I'm all right." I glance back at Irita's retreating form. With the red haze of the planet, she'd be invisible if it weren't for her jumper. "Jutari…I'm worried. Irita said she knew about our plan. Said not to trust Dremmigan."

He straightens and glances over at the gray alien, then

back to me. "It's too late to turn back now."

"But what if—"

Jutari brushes at my cheek, and I realize he's wiping a smudge of dirt away. "It must be today, Chloe. Noku will move you out of the cell tonight, if I am right. I refuse to let him touch you. So even if I must put my faith in Dremmigan, we are going today. One way or another." His voice is low. "The thing to remember is—"

An ear-splitting crackle drowns out his words. The nearest harvester whines and shrieks to a stop, the gears grinding. Smoke begins to pour from the front, and I see people fleeing it on all sides. "Got a jam," someone yells out. "Someone's stuck under the blades!"

A guard rushes forward with his shock-stick in hand, moving past us clumsily as he races through the field.

I look at Jutari, my eyes wide, but he's gazing down the field. I follow his line of sight, and sure enough, Dremmigan is slinking away to the edge of the barrier.

"Time to go," Jutari tells me. Before I can agree, he grabs me and flings me over his shoulder as if I weigh nothing. I swallow my yelp and ignore the slam of my stomach into his plated shoulder. Vomit threatens to come up my throat, and I close my eyes, concentrating on not puking as he races down the field. Because of the low gravity, I bounce against his shoulder even harder, and I grab double fistfuls of his prison uniform to try and anchor myself.

Endless moments pass, and I can tell the second his feet find purchase on regular ground. I squeeze open an eye and see we're near the edge of the barrier. From my vantage point, it looks like nothing more than a glittery shimmer, punctuated by a few metal rods placed strategically in a row. I'm guessing that there's a lot of voltage shooting through that shimmer, though, and shudder at the thought. I don't know how we're going to get through there.

Maybe the guard that's helping us is going to let it down for a short time.

A split second later, I'm set down on my feet, and Jutari touches my cheek. "Stay as close as you can." He grabs my hand and surges forward, and I see we're racing toward a small, camouflaged booth near the edge of the barrier. We step inside, and Dremmigan is there with a bag, talking to a guard. In the distance, I can still hear the whine of the thresher, an endless wave of white noise.

"Got the supplies," Dremmigan says. "You ready to do this?"

Jutari nods.

"It's enough for three days of food and water for one person, or one day for each of you," the guard says. He looks young, his skin a slick, toad-ish sort of green. His gaze flicks to me and then to the others. "Good luck to you. You'll need it. This planet is a death trap."

"Mm." Dremmigan checks the bag and then slings it over his shoulder. He holds a thin, clawed hand out to the guard. "Got a knife?"

The guard immediately pulls one from a sheath at his belt and offers it, blade first, to Dremmigan. "Had to call in a few favors to get this one." He gives me a long, interested look, and my skin prickles. I step closer to Jutari.

"My thanks," Dremmigan says. He reaches to take the knife, but instead of grabbing it, he pushes forward with a surge. The knife buries itself into the guard's chest, and the alien guardsman gives a startled gurgle, then collapses to the ground.

I gasp, horrified. Oh my god.

Jutari's arm goes around me protectively. "He was helping us, fool."

"He was," Dremmigan agrees, bending down to get the knife. He wipes the blade on the guard's uniform and then tucks it into his pack. "And he was far too trusting. The moment someone offered him a better deal, he would have sold us out, and my contacts in-house. Better that he die and keep his secrets." He rummages through the guard's pockets.

I feel sick. There was no need to kill the guard. I think of Irita's words, and I want to get away from Dremmigan as fast as possible.

"There's no time to waste," Dremmigan says, standing. He holds out something that looks like a small wand. "Key to the collars. If you want to save your female, we need to go now."

I look up at Jutari. He seems uneasy, but nods and reaches for the key. "Let us go, then."

I swallow my tears, trying to seem brave. Okay. Okay. I can be strong until we're out of here. Then I can freak out all I want. I stand still as Jutari runs the wand over my shock-collar, and then it falls away from my neck with a hiss. He does the same for his own, and then for Dremmigan. I try not to stare at the gray alien, but I wonder how he's going to view even that simple decision. Jutari picked me over him for something as small as the collars. Am I the next one to be offed because I'm a liability?

I can't think about that. I have to believe in Jutari. He says he wants me forever. I have to trust in that. "How do we do this?" I ask him, rubbing my newly unencumbered neck. "How are we going to get across the barrier?"

"Do you trust me?" Jutari asks, his gaze dark as he focuses on me.

"Of course."

He holds his hand out to me, large and three-fingered and blue. I immediately put my hand in his, reassured by the warmth of his grip and the strength of it.

He won't let anything happen to me.

Jutari presses his mouth to my dirty knuckles, and before I can chide him for that, he picks me up and hefts me over his shoulder again. *Thunk*, and my breath escapes my lungs. "You too, Drem," he calls. "There's no time to waste."

What does he mean, him too? I lift my head to ask, except a moment later I see the tall, slender, smoke-colored alien hang over Jutari's other shoulder. What the heck?

Jutari heads out of the guard shack and toward the barrier. The hair on my head crackles and my body hums with energy. "What are we doing?" I call out. "Waiting for the barrier to go down?"

"No, we're going through it," he tells me.

What?

"Brace yourself, Chloe," Jutari says, his arm tight on my waist. "This will hurt."

That's all the warning I get before he moves forward, and electricity sears through my body. Everything goes black.

CHAPTER 7

JUTARI

THE PAIN OF PASSING THROUGH the barrier is like no other. I groan, staggering forward as the dual weights of Chloe and Dremmigan hang limply off my body. The barrier's not thick, but each step forward feels like an endless one. Then I am through, and I tumble to the ground, weak. My vision is hazy, my skin smells charred, and my hair singed. I'm pretty sure my horns are smoking.

But I'm alive. I take a moment to catch my breath, waiting for my heart to slow down from its panicked racing. Chloe and Dremmigan are both sprawled on the red dirt, and I move to my mate's side, pressing my hand to her breast. Her heart beats. She is well. I touch her bruised face gently and then scoop her gently in my arms and hold her to my breast. I don't believe in deities, but right now, I send a prayer up to whoever might be listening for keeping my Chloe safe.

I take the knife from Dremmigan's pack and gently make a small cut in Chloe's jumper, then into the meat of her arm, hating every drop that she bleeds. I dig the tracker out of her arm, crush it between my fingernails, and then cast it into the dirt. I do the same for my own. With those gone, we'll be difficult to find.

I pick my Chloe up again and hold her close, getting to my feet. She is small, and I do not know how much the barrier will have knocked her out for, so I will carry her. I take the pack from Dremmigan's shoulder and sling it over my back, and then stare down at my "friend."

I don't know what to do. Taking Chloe with me has always been the plan—there's no point in escaping without her. I'm not leaving her behind.

I owe Dremmigan. I should take him with me...but I want to leave him. He used his connections to get us supplies and set up part of the escape but...I'm not pleased. He slaughtered that young, foolish guard just because it was convenient for him. Even when I was at my lowest in my mercenary days, I never killed without necessity. There was always a reason behind it. The bastards I killed were always worse than the ones that hired me. There was always a reason.

There was no reason in that particular slaughter.

Yet if I leave him here, do I put Chloe and myself in danger? If I bring him with us, do I put her in even more danger? Do I break my word even though his was good? To me, at least?

Or do I kill him in cold blood to make things tidy, as he did with the guard? It would be easy to simply pull the breather off his nose and let him choke out, unconscious.

I have never truly trusted him, but now that the choice is mine, I don't know if I can be as coldly ruthless as he was. Perhaps I'm growing weak now that I have a woman to care for. Perhaps I want to be better for her.

It doesn't matter. I can't kill him in cold blood any more than I can leave him behind. I juggle Chloe's limp body against my shoulder and cut the tracker out of his arm. Then

I grab the back of his jumper with my other hand and haul him along, letting his legs drag in the dirt.

I STAGGER ALONG IN THE foothills. In a way, it's good that we're covered in the thick red dirt of the fields - it helps camouflage us from the inevitable search parties that will be heading our way. I'm exhausted, and every bone in my body aches, but I push forward, my pace as brisk as I can go with the two dead weights of my passengers. I need a cave to set them down in, and a place for my fragile Chloe to rest. Under the dark of night, we can continue traveling to a safe spot where I can contact Kivian. For now, the priority is to get away.

The cliffs near the prison are rocky and promising, but they're also too close. It wouldn't matter if there was a cave here, we'd be found instantly. Our best bet is to cover as much ground as possible.

After a short time, Dremmigan groans. I pause and release his jumper, then offer him a hand so he can get to his feet. "You didn't leave me," he grunts, and his breathing sounds shaky. "I'm surprised."

"We had a deal," I tell him. I offer him the pack as a show of trust—even though I have none—and he takes it, pulling it over one shoulder and settling it on his back.

"That hurt worse than I anticipated," he says, rotating one shoulder and then taking a stumbling step forward. "Did your female make it?"

"She did, but she is still unconscious." I tuck her against my shoulder, her face against my neck. "Her body is smaller than ours. It might take time for her to awaken." I don't want to consider that she won't.

Dremmigan nods slowly. "I can walk. Where are we going?"

"We're looking for shelter. Any shelter." I point at distant cliffs, near one of the endlessly churning air-circulators. "I thought we'd head there for tonight. It'll be easier to travel without detection while it's dark."

He nods and rubs his upper arm. "And the trackers?"

"I took them out."

"Glad you thought of it."

Then there's nothing else to say. We stare at each other for a bit, both of us lost in thought. I know what we're both thinking—we're judging if we can trust the other for a bit longer. But I didn't come this far to let Dremmigan ruin things.

And I still have the knife.

So I turn toward the distant cliffs and continue walking.

CHLOE

I'M ALIVE.

It's the first thought that goes through my head as I wake up. Oh sure, everything hurts and I feel like a piece of fried chicken, but I'm alive. I sit up slowly, holding my head as I try to get my bearings. "Mmm…Jutari?"

"Here." A big, familiar body moves next to me, blocking out the little light in the cave. At least, I think we're in a cave. It's dark and hard to tell. A hand touches my cheek, and then something is pushed into my grip. "Drink this."

"Where are we?" I ask as I find the seal on the water pouch and take a sip. Oh man, that's better than I'd expected. I must have been out for a while, because I gulp the entire thing down and I'm still thirsty.

"We're in a cave near the air-circulators, taking a break. Now that the sun is down, we can start moving." Jutari strokes my cheek again. "How do you feel?"

"I'm all right," I lie. Moving is the last thing I want to do right now, but it's not like there's a car waiting to come and pick me up. So I'm just going to have to suck it up for a while. "Are we...did we all make it?"

"Drem is just outside."

Ah. I'm not sure how I feel about that. Feels wrong for me to wish death on him, but at the same time, I can't stop thinking about Irita's warning. I don't want us to come this far to only get stabbed in the back. I get to my feet, taking my time—and the hand he offers me. "Are you okay? How-how did we get away?"

"The shock of the barrier is only slightly stronger than the shock-collars. They have never affected me like most, and so I carried both you and Dremmigan away from the barrier while you were unconscious."

"You did that for us?" I have a knot of gratitude in my throat. "Thank you, Jutari. Are you okay?" As he steps closer to me, I worry. He doesn't look okay. He looks...exhausted. There are dark hollows under his eyes, and his shoulders seem to droop a little. When he pulls me close, he smells like ozone and burned skin, and I stroke his back even as he hugs me against him.

"I am fine."

"You don't look fine," I whisper, not wanting Drem to hear me.

He chuckles a little. "All right. I'm keffing tired. I haven't slept much in the last several days."

"You haven't? Why not?"

Jutari's mouth twitches, and he cups my chin. "I had a sweet female to protect and keep safe from the others in the cell."

Oh. I didn't realize. I feel like a real asshole for not figuring that out until now. "You did that for me?"

"Of course," he says, as if it's the most natural thing in the world to be a sweetheart like that. "So I'm tired and I'd kill for a nap, but right now that's not an option. We need to get farther away from here. We came to the air-circulator to grab some component parts to build a beacon, but Kivian's not going to be able to land here. Not with all the fog this thing is putting out. We need a better location and to get some distance between us and the prison."

"Okay." I'm not convinced, but if that's what he wants to do, he knows better than I do how to survive here. "Who's Kivian?"

"A fellow pirate and someone I trust." He strokes my hair, then runs his knuckles lightly along my cheek. "He's going to be surprised I've settled down."

"No one's more surprised than me," I say dryly. It's true; I never thought I'd find someone at an intergalactic prison of all places, and yet…I'm looking forward to seeing what life has to offer when it's just me and Jutari in a normal situation. One where we can talk and laugh and enjoy each other's company without worrying about the interfering presence of others. One where we can just learn about each other. One where we can spend the entire day in bed without someone else watching.

Yeah, all of that sounds nice. It might be a pipe dream, but it gives me something to look forward to.

I've resigned myself to the fact that I'll never go home. I'll never see Earth again. It's clear that Earth is unfamiliar or off limits to the vast majority of aliens that I've met, and those that know where I'm from regard me uneasily. Unless Jutari wants to take a risk, I won't be going back to my solar system. I won't see Earth's blue skies or hug my friends again. I've known that for a while now.

Funny how it doesn't hurt as much now that I've got Jutari. I no longer feel so terribly alone. I rub a hand briskly up and down his arm, trying to perk his spirits. "All right, so what's the plan? And how can I help?"

His eyes gleam, and I think he's pleased. "The plan is for us to take off now that it is night. We are going to have to cross a great deal of rocky terrain. It's not going to be easy. I can carry you if you're tired."

"I'm good," I reassure him, checking my nose-clip-breather. I'm tired, thirsty, and hungry, but I imagine he is, too. No sense in whining, and I don't want him to feel like he has to carry me. I want to pull my own weight for a change. "What about supplies? And you said you needed parts for a beacon? Do we have everything we need? Should we get backups while we're here?"

Jutari nods. "Good idea. We'll get some extra wiring and a few motherboards while we're here and then head out."

"About time," says Drem from the front of the cave. His voice is flat and emotionless like always, but something about it makes me shiver. I don't like him. I don't trust him.

Something about him sets me on edge, even more than this prison break does.

We set off a short time later, under the dark, nighttime skies. Jutari has a bag full of components that he ripped out of one panel of the air-circulator, and while it all looks like garbage to me, he says he has enough to put the beacon together. I just have to trust him.

I'm glad to put distance between us and the air-circulator, because the air near it is oppressive. It feels thicker than the air on the rest of the planet, heavy with condensation and oppressive. Even though it's dark, we stumble along over the rocky surface. My prison shoes suck, but I don't complain. I'm too worried about the normally graceful Jutari as he staggers forward, his steps occasionally weaving.

He needs a break, but I know I can't suggest it. Something tells me that any sign of weakness in front of Dremmigan would be a bad idea. As we walk, though, I grab a palm-sized rock and hold it in my hand, bringing it with me. Just in case.

At some point during the middle of the night, search-lights appear in the distance, and we huddle—the three of us—against a jagged boulder, watching as patrols begin to sweep the area, looking for us. Jutari's mouth is pulled into a thin line, and I don't think he's happy at their appearance. Maybe he thought we'd have more time.

But the air vehicles don't see us, and the sweep continues past without a peep, and we grab our meager supplies and continue onward.

Dawn is on the horizon when we find a cleft in a large cliff with enough overhanging rock to provide shade through-out the day and protect us from being seen. Jutari collapses against it, eyes immediately closing.

I touch his cheek, frightened. "Are you all right?"

"Just…tired. Need to rest for a few." He tries to manage a half-smile for me, but I can tell he's exhausted.

Dremmigan isn't happy with this development. He crouches next to Jutari and nudges his leg. "Now is not the time to rest."

Jutari puts a hand over his eyes, rubbing them. "I know. I just need a moment."

I want to snarl at Dremmigan. I move protectively in front of Jutari, doing my best to push the other alien aside. "He can take a few minutes to sleep. Leave him alone."

"Now is not the time," Dremmigan states again. "Make your beacon. Call your friend who will rescue us."

"He can do that after he sleeps for a half-hour," I protest.

"No, it needs to be soon," Dremmigan states again. "We do not have enough supplies to last out here for several days."

I'm silent at that, because he's not wrong. We're out of water and food. The supplies Dremmigan's "great" connec-tion brought us weren't much at all when split three ways. Still, I can't help but feel guilty over the fact that Jutari hasn't been sleeping because he's been protecting me. I want to give him the same courtesy. "We'll think of something."

"He needs to make the communicator now," Dremmigan states again. "He can rest when our rescue is on the way."

"Leave him alone—"

"No, it's all right," Jutari says, touching my arm. "He's right. I can relax when the beacon is set up." He sits forward, rubbing his face one more time. "Hand me my bag, Chloe?"

I shoot Drem an angry look and get to my feet, retrieving the bag that Jutari set down a few feet away. The big blue alien takes out pile after pile of components and wires, and I worry that he's not going to be able to make a communicator at all. I wouldn't even know where to begin if it was up to me, and it just makes me exceedingly aware of how dependent I am on others. Never again. If I get out of here, I'm going to learn how to take care of myself.

I watch as Jutari begins to twist wires and attach computer chips, stringing a series of electronic doodads together. It looks like nothing at all to me, but Jutari never pauses, not even when the wind howls through our small canyon and blows grit in our faces. After what seems like forever, he connects a small blue wire to a thing that looks like a knob. A low-pitched whine fills the air, and that slow, confident grin crosses Jutari's handsome face.

"Is that it?" I ask. "Did you do it?"

"It's sending a signal," he tells me with an easy smile.

"Yes, but where is the information it must send?" Dremmigan doesn't look pleased. He gestures at the cobbled-together components that Jutari has cleverly made into something new. "A beacon must have information to transmit."

"I have the information."

"Where, in your mind?" Drem scoffs. "It must be precise if—"

Jutari pulls out the knife. I freeze, wondering what he's

going to do with it, and I'm even more alarmed when he puts the tip inside his mouth. But a second later, he plucks a tiny disk from his tongue and then spits out a mouthful of blood. "Had to keep it somewhere they wouldn't look."

"But...how?" I ask. "They checked everything on me, right down to my fillings." I resist the urge to rub my ACL surgery scar, because I don't trust Drem not to tear me open looking for the screws in my leg.

"It's a special black-market material," Jutari says, wiping at the tiny square. "Made for such occasions." He finds a tiny slot in the makeshift beacon, inserts the chip, and then something begins to spit out an endless string of numbers. "Our location," he says when the computerized voice finishes speaking. "I'm sending this directly to Kivian. Our rescue will depend on what side of the galaxy he's on, of course, but he'll come for us." He leans back and closes his eyes, resting against the rock. The knife hangs loosely in his grip, resting on his lap. "We just have to bide our time until then."

"It is done?" Dremmigan asks. "Nothing further needs to be sent?"

"Done," Jutari agrees, not opening his eyes.

I hold tightly the rock I picked up, suspicious of Drem's constant questions. We're all on edge, I remind myself. It's nothing more than that. But...I don't like the way he keeps eyeing the knife in Jutari's lap. I don't trust him.

But Drem walks away, to the front of the small canyon. And I relax a little. It's just my imagination.

"Chloe," Jutari says, his voice a tired caress. "Come and sleep next to me."

I'm tired, thirsty, and sore. I would love to. But I can't stop thinking about how much sleep he's given up just to protect me. I sit at his side and stroke his arm. "You sleep. I'll watch over you."

He nods without opening his eyes, and I know he's been

pushed to the ends of his endurance. He reaches for my hand, rubbing my fingers. That small gesture is enough to make my heart melt all over again.

Sometimes it's the small things that are everything.

CHAPTER 8

CHLOE

IT DOESN'T TAKE LONG FOR shit to go downhill.

Jutari's been asleep for a short time, his hand on my knee. He sleeps deeply, and while he does, I mentally try to figure out how we're going to make supplies appear out of thin air. I'm racking my brain, trying to remember survival scenarios from reality TV shows. I remember that you can make water appear in the form of condensation even when in a desert, but I don't recall all the details. There was a sheet of plastic involved, and we don't have that, so I'm going to have to think of something else. I pick up Jutari's bag and dig through it to see what we have to work with—

A shadow falls over me from behind.

My skin prickles, and it goes quiet in the canyon. I force myself to remain silent, to act like nothing strange is going on. My heart's pounding with fear, though. Stupid me to turn my back to Drem. Stupid me to leave the knife at Jutari's side because I didn't want to bother him.

I casually slide my hand over my rock, gripping it tight

against my leg. Just let him try something. I'm ready for him. I—

A hand grabs my face from behind. Turns out I'm not ready. Before I can do anything, he's ripped the breather off my nose and flings me aside. I didn't realize he was so strong.

I make a choked sound as I get my first lungful of the unfiltered air. It feels like there's nothing there, and I gasp again, trying to breathe. This is not how I'm going to die! I get on my hands and knees quickly, ready to race over and grab the breather off the ground.

Dremmigan puts his foot down and there's a resounding metallic crunch. He's crushed it underfoot.

Oh shit. This... *is* how I'm going to die. That fucker.

He moves toward Jutari, who's still unmoving and unconscious. Maybe we haven't been loud enough to wake him up yet. Alarm ripples through me as he approaches the big blue alien, and I don't think—I just act.

I grab my rock and slam it down on Dremmigan's foot.

The gray alien howls with pain, knocking me aside with a sweep of his arm. I go flying across the chasm, crashing into a heavy rock. The pain that flashes through me is awful, but I struggle to stay conscious as the black rises at the edges of my vision. He's going to kill me now, I know it. Doesn't matter, because I'm going to choke to death either way. But maybe I can save Jutari.

A blue blur moves through the cave, and I watch, gulping uselessly at the air as Jutari's big body slams into Dremmigan's leaner one. The knife flashes, and Jutari's big hand rises. I close my eyes and don't watch. I can hear it all, though, the wet slam of the blade into Dremmigan's body, his gurgle, and then silence.

"Chloe?"

I open my eyes, panting, to see Jutari. He's gotten to his feet, Drem's still form behind him. The knife in his hand drips with blood, but I don't even care about that. I put a hand to my throat. "Breather," I choke out. "Need his."

"That keffing bastard," he bites out, touching my cheek. He moves to Dremmigan's side, and I wheeze, horrified at how awful this feels. I'm choking to death despite breathing. It's the most helpless I've ever been, and my vision grows fuzzy. What if Drem's breather doesn't fit? What if—

Hands touch my face, and in the next moment, something clips painfully onto my nostrils. "Breathe through your nose," Jutari murmurs. "I've got you."

I inhale deeply—and end up coughing. But it's air, and I spend the next few moments just taking in as much as I can, while Jutari cradles my head in his lap and strokes my hair. When I can breathe without worrying my air is going to disappear again, I give a little sigh and touch his hand. It's stained with a darker shade of something, but I don't even care. "Did you kill him?"

"Yes. Does that disappoint you?"

"Not in the slightest." I inhale deeply again. Pretty sure I can smell Drem on the breather, but pretty sure I also don't care. It's just nice to be able to breathe again. "Bastard tried to take you out while you were sleeping."

"Once I heard him attack you, I feigned sleep to take him off guard." He caresses my cheek, his thumb stroking over my jaw. "Just when your face was no longer discolored, new bruises show up. I am a terrible protector."

"Stop," I whisper, closing my eyes and enjoying his touch. "You were worn out. You're allowed to sleep for a few minutes."

"You did your best to protect me," Jutari says, voice soft. "I am humbled by such actions."

"Of course I did." His praise is making me feel shy. "You looked out for me all those days. The least I could do is not let some asshole murder you."

"You could have let both of us die and then stolen away

when Kivian lands. Or turn Kivian in to the prison authori-
ties." At the disgusted expression on my face, he chuckles. "I
am glad your sense of honor is so strong. It is rare to find
these days."

Sense of honor? Is he crazy? "No sense of honor involved.
I'm happy you pulped his face. I think we're a team. Don't
thank me for valuing your life because I care for you."

He smiles down at me, still stroking my cheek. "My people have a saying…you own my heart, my Chloe."

I beam up at him, forgetting all about the hurts and the
thirst and the borrowed breather I'm wearing. "I don't know
if I'm officially in love yet, because the situation's been too
weird. We've never had a chance to be alone before now. But
I feel things for you. Lots and lots of things. It's just…so soon."

He chuckles. "You are not there yet, but you will be."

Yeah, I suspect I will be, too.

JUTARI

WE DISPOSE OF DREMMIGAN'S BODY, stripping it of what
few items he has and then burying it in the red, sandy soil
a short distance away. No sooner do we cover the last of his
bright skin than another search vehicle flies overhead, leaving us scurrying back to safety. We are both tired and curl
up against each other to wait it out. I must be more tired
than I've imagined, because I fall into a deep sleep, and my
dreams are filled with Chloe. I dream we're stand together
near a wide, open field with no one around but us. Unlike
the terraforming fields, these are tall and lush with golden
grasses and thick crops. She smiles at me, her hand on her
belly, and I feel a sense of utter contentment.

I almost hate to wake up.

When I drift awake, though, I think I'm still dreaming. Chloe sits nearby, her legs tucked under her. She's completely naked, her skin glowing and pale in the strange reddish light of this planet. From where I lie, I can see the dimpled curve of her bottom, the gentle flare of her hips, and the lovely, smooth line of her back. I feel a sharp stab of pleasure at the sight of her, since this is the first time I've been able to truly look my fill at her without the encumbrance of prison clothing. She seems smaller from this angle, and softer, though I'm not sure that's possible. "Chloe?"

She turns to look at me, a hint of a smile on her face. "You're up. Did you sleep all right?"

I still feel as if I could sleep for another two days, but I nod. "No signs of a ship?"

"Nothing yet. No more search parties, either." She gets to her feet, uncurling her legs, and moves forward. As she does, I see that her uniform and Drem's uniform have both been spread flat on the ground, each one covered in rocks. What is she up to? At my curious look, she chuckles and reaches for my hand. "Want to see what I'm doing?"

"Did you not sleep?" I let her take my hand, though I'm more interested in watching her curvy little body than anything else. The sight of her makes my tired body feel rejuvenated, my cock springing to life at the sight of the thatch of curls between her thighs.

Chloe shakes her head at my question. "I was too wound up. I decided to see what I could do to try and make us some water."

"Make us water?" I hope this isn't a human bathroom euphemism.

"Yes! I was thirsty, and I remembered seeing something on survival shows about how if there's a lot of heat and moisture, you can collect condensation on plastic. The air's so muggy here that it has to be carrying a lot of water. Our prison uniforms feel a bit like plastic, so I thought I'd give them a try. It took me a few tries to figure things out. I tried hanging them at first, but that didn't do much except flap in the breeze." She moves to the edge of one of the uniforms spread out on the soil and picks up the rocks holding it down. I notice there's one weighing down the middle and making it dip, and I realize when she pulls the uniform back, it's because it hangs over a large scooped-out hole. At the bottom of the hole is one of our empty water pouches, and she carefully picks it up, then holds it out to me, beaming.

Sure enough, at the bottom of the pouch, there's a tiny bit of water. It's not more than a few sips, but it's water.

"We don't know how long we'll be here, but if we can collect water, we can survive for a bit longer."

I am amazed at the cleverness of my girl. She watches me with an anxious expression, as if looking for approval. I want to grab her and hug her close and tell her just how happy she makes me, but she's holding the precious water. "Drink it," I tell her.

"Oh, but I made it for you. You're bigger than me and probably need it more." She offers it up to me again. "I can wait for the next round."

"And I insist that you drink it," I tell her, fascinated by the gentle swell of her pink-tipped breasts out in the open instead of hidden under her prison jumper.

"Then we should split it," she says firmly. "Because I'm not playing the 'your survival is more important than my survival' game for longer than we have to. The sooner I put this back under there, the sooner it collects more water."

I chuckle and take the small bag when she offers it again. "Very well." I take a precious sip, then another, and then pass it back to her.

She tips the bag back and drains the rest, and then makes a face. "I don't know if I'm disappointed that there wasn't more, or kind of grossed out that it was so warm it's like drinking spit."

"But it is water we did not have, and will make surviving here easier until Kivian arrives."

Chloe bites her lip and gives me a worried look. "You're sure he'll come?"

"I am sure."

"But how can you be so sure?"

"Because he is my brother."

Her eyes go wide with astonishment. "You never said!"

"It never came up. We have gone our separate ways for a long time, but the chip is something we have both had since our youth. It was my father's idea, actually."

"Your father?"

I nod. "He was a rather infamous privateer and wanted us to have a way to escape from anywhere if we got caught."

She just shakes her head, amazed. "There is so much I need to learn about you."

And I about her. But we will have all the time we need once we are free from this hellish planet.

I watch her as she bends down and puts the bag back in the hole, then covers it with the uniform once more. "Here," I say, undoing the neck on my own jumper. "Take mine and we can add it to increase our water."

"Great idea. Bring it over here."

I strip down and watch as she digs another hole in the loose soil, then gently sets the empty bag down at the bottom. At least, I try to. But it's distracting when she's so naked and moving around. Her breasts jiggle as she moves, and her behind has the roundest curve to it that makes my mouth water. By the time she's done and stands up, dusting her hands off, I'm thinking about all the things I want to do to her now that she's mine and mine alone.

And I can't stop thinking about the mouth-on-mouth she

told me about. It breaks all kinds of hygiene laws, but…I cannot say that I'm not intrigued by it. What does it feel like, I wonder. What is the benefit? It must be pleasurable or she would not have suggested it. I'm fascinated at the thought.

She turns around and looks at me, and her gaze grows soft, her lips parting. "What are you thinking about?" She sounds breathless. "You've got a strange look in your eye."

"I was thinking about you and your mouth," I tell her bluntly. "We are alone now, and I would make good on my promise."

"Promise?" Chloe looks flustered. "Oh yes. Our first kiss."

Her reaction fascinates me. I move forward and brush my fingertips over the pink swell of her mouth. "Show me how to do this."

"All right." She bites her lip, and I am drawn to that tiny movement. Her hand moves to my chest, and then she peeks up at me. "You're a bit taller than me, so this might be tricky."

I snort. A bit? I stand nearly two full heads higher than her. "How do humans handle such things?"

"Well, we aren't nearly as tall as you. And when we are, we both sit down together."

Ah. That makes sense. I drop to my knees and extend my arms toward her. "Come, then."

Her cheeks color, and she sidles closer to me, nervous. It's strange, her reaction. Have I not had my hands all over her? Have we not simulated mating over and over again while in the prison cell together? I know intimately how her body feels under mine. I know the sounds she makes when she is going to come. I know the feel of her breasts and her cunt. What is there to be embarrassed over?

Her pale hands move to my shoulders, and she hesitates. "I'm all dirty."

"Do you think that matters to me?" I brush a bit of red dirt off her shoulder and then let my fingers glide down her arm.

"I still want to put my mouth all over you."

Her eyes go soft, and she puts her hands on the sides of my face. She drops to her knees and then wiggles in until she's between my thighs. Then she presses her mouth to mine.

At first, it's just a gentle brush of her lips. Pleasant, but perhaps not worth all the excitement. But then she parts her mouth and her tongue strokes against the seam of my lips, and I feel a jolt rush through my body. I open for her, and her tongue sweeps inside my mouth, rubbing and teasing.

Need explodes through me, and I groan, pulling her closer. My hands lock against her bottom, and she makes a little squeak into my mouth, but does not pull away. Her tongue drags against mine, and she makes another little sound of surprise. I am surprised, too—her tongue is soft and smooth, like her skin. She does not have the ridges on her tongue like my people do. I find that keffing erotic and can't help but stroke my tongue against hers again, enjoying the sensation of our two bodies clashing. Over and over, we do this "kiss," our tongues mating until she is gasping for breath and my cock is aching fiercely. We pull apart, and she gives me a dazed expression.

"Is it always that good?" I ask her, entranced by the slick gleam of her lips.

"No, not always," she says breathlessly, and her gaze moves back to my mouth. I take the hint and pull her back in for another kiss, my hands moving up and down her backside. She has no tail, no protective ridges on her spine. She is nothing but softness, and I can't help but let my hands glide up and down the cleft of her bottom, exploring her. Chloe arches against my touch, and her legs spread farther apart.

I cannot resist the invitation. I stroke my fingers forward, seeking her folds, and find her core, already damp for me. Another groan escapes me at how hot and wet she is, and I want to thrust a finger deep inside her. But the need to give her pleasure drives me even more, and I glide my fingers upward, seeking out the small, sensitive nub that hides in her folds. When I find it, her entire body jerks and she seems to melt against me, her thighs clasping my hand.

"What is this?" I ask between kisses, giving it a little rub. "It is not something our people have."

She rocks against my fingers, a little cry erupting from her throat. "It's...clit..." she pants. "No...biological...purpose. Just feels...good." Her eyes close, and she presses her forehead to mine. "Oh god, does it feel good."

I capture her mouth again and stroke my tongue against hers. "Shall I put my mouth on your cunt? Tease this little bit of flesh with my tongue until you cry out?"

Chloe arches against me, whimpering.

I like to think of that as a "yes." I break our kiss, then move lower and lick the cords of her neck. Even here, she smells soft and sweet. I love the way this fragile human feels in my arms. I must be careful to treat her perfectly, like she deserves to be treated. I cannot be too rough or lose control. All that matters is my Chloe.

I pull her against me and drag one leg and then the other around my waist. When she's clasped around my body, I lean forward, lowering her to the rocky soil. "I should wait to claim you," I murmur even as I dip my head to kiss between the soft globes of her breasts. "But I cannot wait any longer."

"Good," she breathes, her nails digging into my shoulders. "I'm tired of waiting. We're alone, and that's all that matters."

It seems we think alike. I lick the gently rounded surface of her belly, dragging my tongue along her softness. She smells so keffing good—a delicate scent mixed with a hint of sweat and her female musk that makes my senses come to life. I move lower and press my mouth to the soft curls covering her cunt. She moans, squirming with anticipation, and I kiss lower. I cannot wait to taste the nectar from her body. My mouth waters at the thought. I have dreamed of this moment for many days now, and I plan on savoring it.

I push apart the folds of her cunt, reveling in how pink and wet they are. "Look at how you need me," I tell her. "Look at how wet you grow at the thought of my mouth on your cunt." She moans, and I grin to myself, exploring her sleekness with the tip of one finger. The little bud I have teased with my fingertips looks smaller and far pinker up close, and I lean in to taste it.

Her body jerks in response, the breath whooshing out of her lungs. "Oh my god," she moans again. "Your mouth…"

"You want more of it?" I'm happy to comply, tonguing her little "clit" with enthusiasm. When she writhes and makes those fantastic gasping noises, I know she likes it. I lick her a little slower this next time, dragging over the bud so she can feel every ridge on my tongue. "I will give you everything, my Chloe. My human." I love being able to say the words aloud, knowing there's no one around to threaten her.

She's mine for now and forever. I've claimed her fully, and I'm not letting her go.

Her body arches under me, and she reaches forward, one hand going to my hair and the other to one horn. She wraps her fingers around it and then flinches away when I groan. "Was that—was that bad?"

"No," I tell her thickly. "I liked it." And then I continue teasing her clit with my tongue to show her how much I liked it. My horns don't have much sensitivity, but what is there fevers my imagination more than anything. I'm picturing her fingers wrapping around them, tight around their girth, and it makes my cock strain to be buried deep between her thighs.

Chloe's hands grip both horns then, holding my face between her legs, and she pants my name. I give her what she wants, lapping my tongue against her tender clit until she's crying out, shuddering her release. She falls back against the earth, panting and dazed, and I cannot help but watch her reaction, her cunt pink and wet with her orgasm. It entices me and makes my cock tighten. I can wait no longer to be inside her. Grabbing one thigh, I push my body over hers, and it immediately feels familiar. "How many times did we play-act like this?" I tell her, and she moans. "How many times have I covered you, thrusting my cock between your soft thighs? How many times did I hold you close and shudder my need?"

"This time it'll be real, though," she says, breathless. Her eyes are dazed as she gazes up at me, and her hand skims down my chest. "This time I want you deep inside me."

I want that, too. I want it more than anything. I won't let another moment go to waste, either. It's already been far too long a wait to make her mine. I shift my weight, bracing one arm next to her as I use my hand to guide my cock into her warmth. Her cunt is tight, her warmth seeming to suck me in. I push forward, little by little, as Chloe moans underneath me, unable to remain still. She moves her hips, raising them to drive me deeper. She doesn't want me to go slow.

I don't want to go slow, either. With a surge, I bury myself to the hilt inside her.

The gasp that escapes her startles me. Her eyes are wide, as if shocked.

I freeze over her, horrified. "Chloe? Have I hurt you?" The last thing I have ever wanted was to cause her pain. Perhaps I have been too rough. Perhaps—

"W-what was that?" Her hand moves between us, where our bodies are joined. "What's that thing on top of your cock?"

"My spur?" It's not exactly on my cock, but I can't think of anything else she means.

"Yes," she moans, and her eyes practically roll back in her head when I shift my hips. "God, *that* thing."

"You do not like it?"

"It's hitting my clit," she says with a whimper. "I might like it too much."

Relief rushes through me, and I chuckle. It will take time for us to learn each other's bodies and ways. For now, I am just glad that I am not hurting her. "Do you want me to get off you?"

"Fuck no." She arches her hips again, then gasps. "I want you to *move*."

My sweet, pushy human. I thrust forward, and Chloe gives a low little scream.

"God, ridges, too? This is so fucking unfair." Her nails dig into my skin, and when I thrust again, her cries grow louder.

This time, I recognize that the sounds are those of pleasure, and I hold on to her hip, rocking into her again. I find a pace and push into her, using my hips to power each thrust. Over and over, I sink into her tight, slick heat. Nothing has ever felt better than this. She grips me like a vise, her cunt hugging my length. With every thrust, Chloe gets more and more aroused until she's wailing my name, and her entire body shudders underneath mine with the onset of another orgasm. Her pleasure only heightens mine, and when my sac tightens, I welcome the release of my seed and let my spend flood into her.

Stars flash before my eyes, and I come so hard that I feel as if I've poured my entire body into hers. If I died right in this moment, I would be a happy male.

Drained, I collapse on top of my small female, and then somehow find the strength to prop my tired body up over hers so I do not crush her. Panting, our breathing mingles, and I scan her face to make sure that the breather remains in place on her small nose. "Are you all right?"

"Oh yeah," she says dreamily. "I'm what you would call 'better than all right.'"

My Chloe has such a pleased look on her face that I

cannot help but grin. I lean in and nuzzle her nose, then decide to give her a light kiss. Her hair is tangled around her face and the silvery translator bulb in her ear, and I push the dark locks away. "We'll get rid of this thing on the ship," I tell her. "Kivian's got a lot of high-tech equipment. You can have a chip inserted into your neural pathways instead of having to deal with this cheap garbage."

"Is that what you have?" she asks with a yawn. "Is it hard to do?"

"It is one of the most basic procedures." I trace her small ear. "And it will free this up so I can gaze upon my mate's beauty unencumbered."

"Sounds good to me." She has a sleepy smile on her face. "I was wondering how you knew so much English."

"Eng-lish?" I vaguely remember hearing that word before, when the settings in my chip changed over. "Is that where you're from? Your homeland is Eng-lish?"

"Nah. My home's America. English is just the language." She yawns and then pats my arm. "You'd probably like Earth. It's nothing like this shithole."

I chuckle. Shit-hole is a perfect way of describing Haven. "If it is different from this place, then yes, I would probably like it." I hesitate. I…should ask if she wishes to stay or if she wants me to take her home. I know it is the right thing to do, but the thought of giving her up fills me with a possessive, ferocious anger.

"You okay? You're squeezing me a little tight." She wiggles underneath me.

I hadn't even realized. "You…" I clear my throat, then gather my courage. "My brother will be arriving with his ship soon. I am sure we can figure out how to get you back to your planet, one way or another. Would you…would you like that?"

Her eyes open, and she blinks at me. "You…can?"

I nod. It is the most difficult thing I have ever had to do, that simple nod. If her planet is forbidden, Kivian won't be happy, but I can talk him into it. Piracy and raiding is in our blood. Nothing is off limits to people like us. At least, not for long.

She swallows hard. Her eyes grow suspiciously shiny. "Are you—are you trying to get rid of me, Jutari?"

What? "Never," I say fiercely. I grab a handful of her silky hair, as if that will somehow tie her to me forever. "But I want you to be happy, even if it's not with me."

"I want to stay with you." Her arms go around my neck, and she squeezes, pulling me in until I fall against her. "You're mine and I'm yours, okay?"

"Chloe…there is nothing I want more than that." I stroke her soft, soft skin. "But I am a criminal. I cannot live freely. It'll mean hiding out for the rest of our lives—"

"I don't care. I want to stay with you. There's no life for a human in your world anyhow. To them, I'm a freak show."

She speaks the truth. A human would be treated as an oddity…even if they let her live. After what I have been told of her history, I don't even know if that's possible. "Which is why I could take you home—"

"So…what? I can just forget the last month of my life? Like I haven't been changed completely? Like I haven't met you? I'll just go back to a job working at a shoe store and act like nothing happened?" A watery little laugh bubbles up in her throat, and I realize she's on the verge of tears. "I'm not the same girl I was, Jutari. I've killed people. I lived in a prison. I met you. I don't care if it means we're spending the rest of our lives on some backwater planet, as long as we're together, all right?"

"All right," I say softly, and bury my face against her neck. Never have words been sweeter to hear. If she had wanted to leave I…it startles me to realize that I would have let her go.

Funny how the selfish bastard I used to be is completely gone. The ruthless killer Jutari, assassin and mercenary, has been brought low at the thought of a female's tears. I want nothing more than to make Chloe happy.

She sniffs hard. "Wh-what's that, Jutari?"

"What's what?" I ease off of her, stroking her dirty hair away from her face.

She points overhead, and I sit up, looking up.

A spaceship's lights are flickering overhead. I freeze, squinting at the reddish winds that howl and obscure everything with a fine scarlet glaze. As the ship comes in closer, I relax. It's not a prison transport.

It's Kivian.

I lean in and press another kiss to Chloe's mouth. I am already addicted to the taste of her. "We should dress quickly. I don't want my brother getting a look at what's mine."

Her eyes light up. "We're rescued?"

EPILOGUE

CHLOE

I RUB MY ROUNDED BELLY as I gaze out at the fields of our farm. Jutari should be coming in for the day soon, and I'm eager to see him. I want a foot rub, a shoulder rub, and a kiss, not necessarily in that order. It's been a long but successful day, and I gaze around my small kitchen with pleasure. Three hundred cans of jitai berry jam and a hundred sixteen loaves of protein bread that can be vacuum sealed into tiny nuggets and will last for years. Yesterday was seski pickles, a savory sort of vegetable I've learned to love. Farming—even in outer space—is all about canning and making the food last so you don't have to worry about your next meal. There's a quiet sort of joy in seeing a stocked pantry, and this time it's no different than the last time we harvested and made supplies for the long winters on Risda III.

Well, no, I take it back. Last winter I wasn't pregnant. Last winter, we'd sent off for a "frontier" doctor to come and visit our homestead out on the far reaches of the known galaxies. He'd arrived and shot me full of hormones that would allow my body to recognize and accept Jutari's sperm and for us to have a child.

Now here we are, almost a full Earth-year later (and two-thirds of a Risda year), and my belly's finally bulging out and I'm getting past the barfs that come with the first trimester of normal human pregnancy. Jutari's people—the messakah—seem to be pregnant for a long, long time, so we're not exactly sure when this baby will be coming, but it'll be baking for a while longer. That's all right by me—I'm enjoying being pregnant (now that I'm not puking all the time), and I'm enjoying the closeness it's brought Jutari and myself.

I never thought I'd love my big blue guy so freaking much. Even now, just thinking about him makes me sigh happily. I peek out the window to see if he's coming home, and my heart races when I see a familiar pair of broad shoulders and arched horns heading in through the fields. He's home.

I move to the front panel of our house and push the button that opens the "portal," though I'll always think of it as a front door. Our home is a little domed construction that's thermoregulated even in the heat of summer and the cold of winter, and it's not huge, but I like its coziness. Since I'm pregnant and can't work in the field with Jutari (I think my protective guy would have a heart attack at the thought) I've worked on making our home more pleasant. I've gotten yarn from a neighboring farm that raises goat-like fluffy creatures, and my mom taught me how to crochet years ago, so I've been busy making blankets and wall hangings and anything else I can imagine.

Jutari's broad face lights up at the sight of me coming out to greet him, and it's like we're newlyweds all over again, even though we've been "mated" for almost two years now. His steps pick up until he reaches my side, and then he grabs me in his arms, lifts me off my feet, and nuzzles my neck. "My sweet wife. I missed you."

"I missed you, too." I wrap my arms and legs around him and hold tight. "How's the farming?"

He presses a kiss to my mouth, and his hands slide to my butt, holding me against him. "Good. The kachas got into the beans again, but Goros says he'll give us two of their young when they're weaned in exchange for what we've lost."

"They're good neighbors," I agree, thinking of Goros's nearby farm, and kiss my Jutari again. "You upset?"

"Not at all. My little human has mentioned how much she likes kacha milk, so I thought it would be good to have a few of our own." He grins at me. "I hope you are ready to tend animals."

"Well, I clean up after you, so I figure if that hasn't trained me, nothing will."

"That so?" He mock-growls, and nibbles at my neck, making me squeal. I love how playful my big blue husband is. I'd have never thought that the big, fierce, blue alien in maximum security at an intergalactic prison could be fun, but he's got a devilish side to him that comes out, especially around me.

"It's totally the truth," I call out as he enters our small house and heads straight for our bed. He's sweaty and a little dirty from working out in the fields all day, but that doesn't bother me one bit. Our playful banter ends as I press my mouth to his in a deep kiss, and then the kiss becomes something more.

A lot more.

After we've had sex, Jutari puts one blue hand on my rounded belly, caressing it. "How is my son today?"

"Mmm, busy. He's been bouncing against my bladder all morning." I put my hand over his. "You think he'll come out with horns?"

"Messakah children do, but this one will be half-human." His expression grows unnaturally serious, and he gazes up at me. "Are you happy here? With me?"

I tilt my head at him. "That's an odd thing to ask."

He rubs his thumb over my belly, sending skitters through my still-sensitive body. "I just…worry that you will not be happy here. We are very far away from the nearest space station. We don't get many visitors. It's just you and me, and soon there will be a child to think about. I worry this is lonely for you, Chloe. I want you to be happy."

"I *am* happy," I reassure him. "Did I think I was going to grow up and become a space farmer? No. Did I think I was going to marry a notorious criminal and live on the edge of the galaxy in hiding because he's wanted for a list of crimes and I'm a freakish alien? No." His expression grows bleaker with every word I speak, but I continue. "But am I happy? Absolutely." I reach up and touch his cheek. "I love being here with you. I love our little farm. I don't mind that we don't have many neighbors—it makes me feel safer that way, because no one's going to come and take me away from you. I don't mind that we only get a few visitors a year, and it's usually your brother and his new wife. I don't mind farming. I don't mind any of this. It doesn't matter that it's not an exciting life. I think I had enough exciting back on Haven. I'm ready for nice and quiet."

He grins, showing off his sharp white teeth that look so dangerous and are yet so very gentle against my skin. "I feel the same."

Our baby chooses that moment to kick against his daddy's hand. "See?" I tell Jutari. "We're in complete agreement."

AUTHOR'S NOTE

DEAR EVERYONE,

THANK YOU SO MUCH FOR reading! I know this isn't our beloved sa-khui tribe, but the moment Chloe was mentioned in Kate's book, I immediately had a story for her. I even dreamed about it. So of course I had to write it!

Is this going to be an ongoing series? I don't know that it will. I do think I've left Chloe and Jutari in a happy place. I have stirrings for Kivian's story (he deliberately doesn't show up on screen in this book because I want to give myself room to play) but beyond that, this might just be a side-jaunt into fun territory and nothing more.

If this is your first book of mine you've ever read, welcome! I hope you enjoyed!

For those of you who are long-time fans of the barbarians, the next book to come out will be Summer's story - we'll be going back to the ice planet and exploring what's happening there. And if you've read Fireblood Dragons, well, you saw a hint I dropped and are probably wondering about that. Wouldn't you like to know? *g*

At any rate, this was a story that just had to come out, and it was a lot of fun to write, prison and all. I hope you enjoyed it just as much as I did!

See you next time! <3

Ruby

WANT MORE?

For more information about upcoming books in the Ice Planet Barbarians, Fireblood Dragons, or any other books by Ruby Dixon, 'like' me on Facebook or subscribe to my new release newsletter.

Thanks for reading!

<3 Ruby

Made in the USA
Columbia, SC
09 July 2024

38408407R00081